# The Chronicle... ld

MW00933882

## Mouse

## Book 4

# "Timothy the Cotton Field Mouse"

By

William Fontana Sr., M.A.

©2012 TXu 1-864-430

ISBN-13: 978-1493619979

ISBN-10: 1493619977

# Table of Contents

## About the Interactive nature of this book:

Reading a book can be a pastime. Because of the potential for activity in a digital book, in the "Cotton Field Mouse" I have provided opportunities for the reader to become engaged with the content. Many of the illustrations have hidden objects and messages that can be discovered by enlarging areas of the illustrations. Also, at the end of the book, the reader will find the *interactive guide.* This *guide* enables the reader to become more involved with the chapters of the book by using the Internet to visit relevant web sites to locate images and information that pertain to the chapter. With each chapter the interactive guide encourages the making of images that are inspired by the cotton field. These images can then be posted at https://www.facebook.com/Timothy the Cornfield Mouse on the *Facebook* page of the first Timothy the Field Mouse book, "Timothy the Cornfield Mouse." By doing so, the reader can join the Timothy community by sharing their own talents with the world and enrich the magical culture of the organic cotton field where Timothy and Timothina live. My hope is that by making the Timothy books more interactive, the readers will not only be able to visit the fields where Timothy lives through the magic of reading but also they will be able to take up residence there through the activities that are suggested.

# Credits

Barbara Minor for proofreading and many helpful suggestions to improve the book.

My daughter Amelia for her spirit, imagination and love of animals. Her imagination has provided us with the inspiration for all of the Timothy books.

My son Will for his great passion to help in any way that he can. He has been very helpful in making the cover design, improving illustrations, and working on technical issues, and now he is engineering the Timothy interactive games.

Mark Foster, a friend and San Joaquin Valley farmer who has written out the cotton growing sequence notes for me and has also answered my questions about cotton farming. He has also been very informative to talk to about animal interactions on the farm.

Illustrations were made using Serif software: www.serif.com/

Some websites that are relevant in a general way in growing organic cotton:

http://foxfibre.com/

http://www.ota.com/organic/mt/organic_cotton.html

http://www.sustainablecotton.org/

http://www.organic-cotton.us/

http://www.5min.com/Video/What-Are-the-Benefits-of-Using-Organic-Cotton-516985841

http://www.youtube.com/watch?v=aJs7KZtyxus

http://en.wikipedia.org/wiki/Organic_farming_methods

http://farmhub.textileexchange.org/upload/library/Farm%20reports/Crop%20diversification.pdf

Find the green cross.

# Mouse Dream

As Timothy slept on his green jade cross, he began to dream. He was now in a field of tall plants. He could tell that the tall plants were very different from any plants he had ever seen before.

He was looking for something, not really understanding what it was. He found a field mouse who was all black. He asked the black field mouse if she could help him find what he was looking for, but the black mouse ran away and did not answer. He ran after the black field mouse but could not catch her. He was running and running, trying to catch up, but it was no use; she was too fast.

It was then that Timothy realized the plants that he was chasing the black mouse through were all white. He was chasing a black field mouse through a field of white.

Find the black field mouse of Timothy's dream.

Then it happened. *He saw his mother.*

He ran to her. He was so happy to see her.

Timothy woke up to the sound of tlot, tlot, tlot. The wise old pheasant was outside of his burrow, just beyond the blackberry bush. Timothy ran out to talk to the wise old pheasant.

"Wise old pheasant, why are you here?" Timothy asked.

The wise old pheasant replied, "I wanted to see that you made it back to our farm."

"I returned right after you," Timothy said. Then went on, "I had a strange dream."

"What did you dream, Timothy?" the wise old pheasant asked.

"I was chasing a girl mouse through fuzzy, white plants," Timothy replied.

The wise old pheasant began to tremble. Timothy noticed that the bird was shaking. "Why are you trembling?" Timothy asked.

"Because I am afraid of what your dream means," the pheasant replied.

"Is it the fuzzy white plants that make you afraid?" Timothy asked.

"Yes," replied the pheasant. "Those fuzzy white plants are cotton plants."

"Why are you afraid of cotton plants?" Timothy asked.

"Cotton is a very different crop, Timothy. The giants grow cotton for their extra skins. A cotton field always brings lots of turmoil and changes. Also, the giants try to kill me."

"Why do they want to kill you?" Timothy asked.

"It is a long story probably best left for a later time," replied the pheasant.

# Animal Prejudice

Timothy was lonely. He waited and waited for the giants to burn the wheat stubble, but the fire never came.  Instead the wheat stubble field became a field of mixed plants when the rains came.  Timothy was excited and relieved because he understood that the giants had decided to let the field go fallow.

The new plants were coming up like crazy, and there was a fantastic variety.  The wheat field stubble was decomposing thus adding nutrients to the sweet earth to nurture the new plants.  Also, the stiff stubble provided shade, so that the ground remained moist for the new plants.

Soon there was enough cover for Timothy to forage in the fallow field, hidden from the predators.  Timothy loved the taste of the wild oat plants and the wheat plants that germinated from the leftover wheat seeds.

The little wildflowers also enthralled Timothy and he loved the taste of the wild mustard.  He discovered the secret of the Blue Dicks.  He could dig down to their roots and find the tasty bulbs.

Timothy was digging feverishly, and he had absentmindedly forgotten to watch for predators when he heard the powerful wings.  He tried to run but it was too late!  He braced for death.

When he dared to look, he saw Gerald. Gerald tilted his head to the right, then to the left, and then he touched his beak to the ground.

"You need to be more careful, little one," Gerald said.

"I am sure glad to see that it is you, Gerald," Timothy replied.

"How have you been, Timothy?" Gerald asked.

"I have been just fine, but a little lonely since Cindy mouse left," Timothy answered.

"So the girl mouse left you?" Gerald said.

"Yes, and I am a little concerned about something the wise old pheasant said," Timothy went on.

Gerald then said, "I am sorry that you are alone now, Timothy, I know what that is like."

There was a long pause, then Gerald said, "The wise old what?"

"The wise old pheasant," Timothy replied.

Gerald ruffled his feathers and shook his head back and forth. Timothy could tell that he was very agitated.  "What's wrong, Gerald?" Timothy asked.

"I just can't believe that an intelligent mouse like you would be talking to the likes of a pheasant," Gerald said.

Timothy countered, "The wise old pheasant is a good friend and also very wise."

"Timothy, I thought that you were smarter than that; I just can't believe that you would be friends with a pheasant," Gerald said.

Timothy sensed that there was something dreadfully wrong with the feelings that Gerald had for the wise old pheasant.  He also did not want to make the crow more upset, but he did manage to ask, "Why don't you like the wise old pheasant?"

"It is not just me; crows, in general, do not like pheasants.  They are fat, less intelligent, and they have color! Oh, and lest I forget, they can hardly fly. They steal our forage. They are aliens.  They were brought here by the giants, and they do not belong!"

Timothy was stunned! How could this be? He thought that all of the animals respected and appreciated the wise old pheasant. He wanted to defend his friend, but he felt it was wiser to just let things be since Gerald was so upset.

Find the edible Blue Dick bulbs.

Timothy just sat there looking at Gerald; then he said that he was trying to dig up the Blue Dick bulbs. Gerald said, "I like the bulbs of the Blue Dick as well." Gerald then scratched and pecked until he found one of the savory bulbs.  He took it in his beak and flew away.

Timothy was upset and confused.  He did not know what to do about one of his friends disliking his other friend.   He also wondered anew about the giants. He remembered the little American sparrow and what it had said about the English sparrow, and now, again, he heard about an animal that did not belong and was introduced by the giants. He decided to just keep things to himself for awhile until he could sort it all out, but he made up his mind to find out more about why Gerald had called his friend an alien.  He wanted to know exactly what it meant to be an alien.

Find the hidden mouse.

# Timothy Finds His Mother

The fallow field was even better than the one he had known as a tomato field mouse. It had been months since the giants had done anything to their field, and there was a plethora of plant and insect varieties. The rains had been plentiful, and the fallow field grasses and wildflowers grew taller and taller.

Timothy was foraging for tender plant stems, wild flowers and insects.  It was easy to stay concealed from predators in the fallow field.  He found his old friend Freddy the rabbit, and they had another rabbit run and mouse chase game.

It was near sundown when Timothy, returning to his burrow, noticed a small animal in the grass ahead of him.  He wondered if it could be a mouse that he knew, possibly Cindy.  He approached the little animal cautiously with his whiskers twitching.  Then he caught the scent of the animal.  He suddenly became more excited than he could imagine.  *That was the scent of his mother!*

A mouse never forgets its mother's scent.  He rushed to see her.  When he broke through the grass wall to where she was, he was bounding with joy.  He ran right to her and touched her nose.  She seemed less excited to see him than he was to see her.  In fact, she was not excited at all.

"Mom, Mom, it's me, Timothy."  He said it again and again.

Finally she said, "Timothy, you have grown to be a fine young mouse.  It is good to see you again."

"Mom, Mom, I thought that you were killed by the flood." Timothy said.

His mother replied, "No, son, I can swim very well, and your warning came just in time for me to push out my mouselings, and we all made it safely to high ground.  But with our burrow gone and the mouselings nearly grown, we all eventually went our separate ways."

Timothy then told his mother that he had found his brother and that they had been together for awhile, until the terrible machine nearly killed him and he lost track of his brother.

Somehow, though, it seemed as if his mother was keeping something from him, but he just could not figure out what it was.  Finally, after foraging together for awhile, Timothy asked his mother if she would like to come back to his burrow with him.  He told her about his wonderful piece of jade and made his burrow sound as pleasant as he possibly could.

His mother seemed distracted, and finally said, "No thank you, Timothy, but if you return here tomorrow, we can forage together again."

Timothy was disappointed, but he was heartened by the hope of seeing his mother on the morrow.

Timothy slept very little that night.  He was so anxious to be with his mother again.  When the morning came, Timothy was out in the fallow field early, looking for his mother.  He returned to the same place where he had seen her the day before and waited.  He had just about given up hope that she would return when he heard a soft mouse voice say, "Timothy, is that you?"

He ran up to his mother and nuzzled her.  He was so happy to be with her again that he forgot about anything else.  They foraged together.  They even played a little together.  Timothy could not remember when he had been so happy.  His mother did seem a little distracted, but he just shook it off and pretended that everything was as it was when he was a mouseling.

He told his mother about all of the things that had happened to him since they were separated.  He told her about Cindy mouse and how they had had mouselings together.  He told her about how the mouselings had left and how he hoped to see some of them again.  He then told her about the troubles that he and Cindy had and why she left him.  His mother listened carefully to Timothy's stories.

She finally said, "I don't think Cindy mouse was the right mouse for you, Timothy.  You need to find a more adventuresome mouse who can keep up with you."

For many days, Timothy would join his mother in the fallow field.  They always met in the same place that only a mouse could find.  It was a bare area of ground, in the otherwise verdant field, that had an especially nice odor to it. From the very first meeting in the fallow field, their relationship began to change. They became more like equals with a great deal of respect for each other.  Timothy really loved his mother and was so grateful to be back together with her.  However, there was always something that she seemed to be keeping from him, but he did not want to disturb their good times by pressing her to find out what the mystery was.

It was after a great time of foraging together that Timothy finally got the nerve to ask his mother if she would come to his burrow to see his wonderful jade cross.   He was so surprised when she said, "Yes."

When she entered his burrow and saw the green jade cross, she tilted her head to the side (the way animals do when they are confused).   Then she said, *"Timothy, this does not belong here or with you.  This piece of jade belongs to one of the giants. It is a giant's thing, and you really have no business keeping it."* Timothy was surprised; he did not know what to think.  He had always considered the jade cross to be his.  He had never really contemplated anything else.

He explained to his mother how he had found it and how it made him feel less lonely.  She seemed to patiently listen, but then she said, *"Timothy, we live in a world apart from the giants.  It is never good to try to mix their world with ours.  It always comes to no good."*

After a while she said that she had to go, but before she left, she said, "Timothy this green jade cross makes me feel very uneasy."

Timothy was beginning to feel very lonely.  He had lost Cindy.  He had found his mother, but she didn't understand how important his piece of jade was to him.  He was starting to wonder if the fear that the wise old pheasant had of cotton might have some merit.

The next morning, though, Timothy's mother was at their favorite spot waiting and he felt much better upon seeing her.  Timothy found that his mother was an excellent talker and she would talk to him about anything.  Upon learning of the other creatures in Timothy's life, she spent time discussing each one.

Of the most interest to her was Gerald.  She told Timothy that he was of a special nature.  She told him that sometimes animals have a joint purpose in life and that Gerald was an ally in a joint purpose. She was amazed by the stories of the wise old pheasant and the counselor rat.  She told Timothy that she had never met such animals and that he must indeed have a special purpose in life and that she was proud to have him for a son.

Timothy's mother did not chastise him the way that Cindy did, but Timothy could tell that she had some of the same concerns about his life that Cindy did. As time went on, Timothy began to rely more and more on his mother for advice and also mouse teamwork.

Timothy could tell that his mother was getting old by the grey fur around her face. She was still very fast and agile in spite of her age.

Probably meeting in the same place every day was not such a good idea. One night, when Strand the red fox was following his nose, scenting for field mice, gophers, or any other prey animal in the fallow field, he found the scent of a mouse that he remembered very well. At last he had found the scent of the magical mouse. Oh, how that scent brought back memories.

Strand had gone over in his mind again and again his attempts to catch and eat the magical mouse. The mouse with such power had to be his ultimate prey animal. And now he had caught the scent again. He could tell from the scent that there were two mice. He could also tell from how often they had met, that they were happy together. He was reminded of the time he tried for the two-mouse meal. It was all coming back to him, the frustration and the mystery of the magical mouse escapes. He could determine from the scent the approximate time the two mice were together.  He could also tell that this was a meeting place of theirs. He made up his mind to wait for them to return, and this time he would catch and eat only the magical mouse.

Find how focused Strand is on his prey animal.

Dreams of his future magical power were dancing through his mind as he lay hidden in the deep grass of the fallow field.

The sun was just coming up when Timothy's mother arrived at their meeting place and began to forage, totally unaware of the menace hiding a short distance away. When Timothy arrived, they touched noses, as they always did, and then set off to forage together.

Timothy's mother said, "Son, it is a beautiful day, and I am glad to be with you again."

Timothy responded by saying, "I love you, Mom and I am so happy that I found you."

Strand listened and thought, "Enjoy it while you can because soon there will only be one of you alive, or on second, thought maybe you will be together forever in the *spirit world*. And I will be the magical fox!"

He waited without moving a muscle for just the right moment to begin his lightning quick strike. He just wanted Timothy.

The mice were getting closer and closer. When they were within striking distance, he noticed something that was a distraction. One of the mice was quite old, and predators have a rule to take the old animal, or less capable animal, first. He would have to violate this rule if he was to target Timothy the magical mouse, because Timothy was younger and stronger.

Strand was greedy for power, and he had become obsessed with getting revenge. *He would violate the rule.* Everything was just right for the attack except for one small detail.

The dew was especially heavy on the plants on this morning, and dew droplets can be like little convex mirrors. Timothy's mother was standing on her hind legs, trying to reach an especially good looking mustard flower, when she saw Strand reflected in the dew drops above her.

Can you find Strand reflected in the dew drop?

She acted out of motherly instinct. She dropped to all fours and ran between Strand and her son. Strand made his pounce, but right in front of him was that old mouse. He couldn't help himself; he grabbed her in his mouth.  Then he realized that he had made a mistake and dropped her so he could get Timothy.  She let out a warning squeak, and Timothy ran so quickly through the fallow field, his little mouse body became invisible in the thick growth of plants.

As Strand bounded through the fallow field looking for Timothy in vain, he became even more convinced of the power of the magical mouse, and oh, how he wanted that power.  *The mouse had disappeared again!*

# Ripping

Timothy returned to their meeting place in the fallow field, but, somehow, he knew he was alone again. He waited and waited for his mother to return, but she did not come back.  He realized after awhile that she never showed him where her burrow was, so he could not try to find her.  Timothy gave up after awhile and started to forage alone.

The birds had returned to the fallow field for seeds and insects.  When the rains came, the robins would come to listen for worms.  Goldfinches and sparrows were often about.  And from time to time, Timothy could hear the wonderful call of the meadowlark. Killdeer would land and run at the edges of the field. Their call reminded Timothy of the call of the meadowlark. The fallow field was alive with plants, insects, mammals, and birds.  What a wonderful place for a field mouse.  *Timothy wished that it could remain wild and free forever.*

The sun was just barely up, and Timothy was returning to his burrow when he heard the powerful machine start.  He was very curious and wanted to see what this machine looked like, so he loped through the grass toward the sound.  When he saw the machine, he was amazed.  It was huge!  It had tracks instead of wheels and was pulling a ripping plow.  When the ripping of the fallow field, started the whole ground shook.

The huge machine was literally tearing apart the ground.  The blades were sinking in to a depth of four feet!  Timothy was terrified by what was happening to the fallow field; everything was being torn apart by the powerful plow.  He couldn't help but remember how the wise old pheasant trembled at the thought of the cotton field, and now he was trembling also. Timothy ran for the hedgerow. When he was safely in the hedgerow, he watched in amazement.

The machine pushed its way across the field in a very straight line, dragging a marking plow off to the side of the ripping plow so that the tractor could return on exactly the same line, following the path of the marking plow. Timothy had learned a long time ago not to put his burrow in the open field, but he felt sorry for the animals that had nests and burrows in the path of this machine. He hoped that his mother's burrow was safe out of the path of the machine.

While he was looking out from the hedgerow, he saw many animals fleeing from the massive machine.

Suddenly the hedgerow was becoming very populated. The birds got out of the way of the tractor with ease, but for other animals, it was not so easy. Hiding in the hedgerow was all that was left for many of them.

Timothy remembered what the wise old pheasant had said about change, and he tried to think of what was happening in a positive way, but it was very difficult in view of the fact that that huge machine was literally tearing apart the fallow field that he loved so much. Timothy needed some help here to try to understand what was happening; he needed to talk to the wise old pheasant.

Timothy was sure that the wise old pheasant would have fled the havoc that was ensuing. So he was very surprised to find his old friend in his favorite roost near his own blackberry bush. "Tlot, tlot, tlot," the wise old pheasant greeted Timothy.

"Wise old pheasant, what is going on?" asked Timothy.

Amazingly, the wise old pheasant seemed very calm. He answered Timothy in an almost unconcerned way, *"Timothy, the giants plow like this from time to time so that the water will get deeper into the ground. For cotton plants, that is very important because the plants sometimes go a long time without water, and the deep watering allows the water to remain longer in the soil. Except for the* pocket gophers with shallow tunnels, all of the animals will be fine."

Find the fleeing Freddy rabbit. For what reason could Lucina's mom be getting off of the ripping tractor?

Timothy felt better already. He was so glad to have as a friend the wise old pheasant.

Unexpectedly, the wise old pheasant went on, "It will be interesting to see how the giants prepare the soil and plant the cotton. If I could say that there was a better time for me in the cotton field, it would be now."

Timothy just had to ask, "Why?"

"Because the giants never try to kill me while they are preparing the field to grow cotton," the wise old pheasant said.

"Why do the giants try to kill you?" Timothy asked.

"I do not know, I just know that when the cotton has been harvested, they come after me and my kind with dogs and guns," the wise old pheasant answered.

"Are guns what they used to scare away the birds from the newly planted wheat field?" Timothy asked.

"Yes," replied the wise old pheasant.

"How do you escape?" Timothy asked.

"I have been lucky so far; they want me to fly when their dogs find me but I never do. I always run. I can run very fast. When I run, they are surprised and they miss me with their shot," the wise old pheasant answered.

Timothy was now aware that the crows hated the wise old pheasant and the giants wanted to kill him. He asked himself, "How could this be?"

*He loved the wise old pheasant and could not imagine how his life would be without him. He just had to try to understand what was going on with his friend. His native field mouse curiosity was piqued to the maximum.*

Timothy decided to question the wise old pheasant about something he had never asked before. He wanted to understand his friend and the things that made life so difficult for him.

"Wise old pheasant, I was talking to my friend Gerald the crow and I mentioned you," Timothy said.

The wise old pheasant interrupted, "You were talking to a crow?"

"Yes, he is a friend of mine," Timothy replied.

"Timothy, I did not know that you were a friend of crows. They are horrible animals they attack us and steal our eggs." the wise old pheasant stated.

Timothy was surprised that the crows were stealing pheasant eggs. This account of conflict just seemed to worsen as it went. He felt very insecure about proceeding to find out more about the hatred that existed between the crows and the pheasants because he didn't want to lose the friendship of either Gerald or the wise old pheasant. Timothy was in the middle of something that had been going on a long time, and he wasn't at all sure that he could do anything about it. Timothy was at another crossroad; he could simply keep quiet and hope that his friends would forgive him for his associations. Or he could try to change their feelings toward each other and maybe risk both of their friendships.

Timothy decided that he needed to investigate what was behind the hatred before he could possibly do anything about it. "Wise old pheasant, I do not know what an alien is," Timothy informed him.

"An alien is someone who comes from a different place and does not belong. Sometimes they come on their own, and sometimes they are forced to come to a new location."

"Are you an alien?" Timothy asked the wise old pheasant.

"Why do you ask, Timothy?"

"Because Gerald called you an alien," Timothy said.

"I guess the crow is right about that. We were brought here against our will."

"Why?" Timothy asked.

"The giants like our colorful feathers, and they also like to hunt us with their dogs."

"Is that what you meant about them trying to kill you?"

"Yes, when the cotton plants are dry, they come with their dogs to try and kill me; they have tried many times," The wise old pheasant answered.

"Where did you come from?"

"It was a long time ago, and all that I know about where we came from was my mother called it the land of jade on the other side of the ocean," the wise old pheasant answered.

Timothy told the wise old pheasant about his wonderful piece of jade and all that it meant to him, and then he asked," What's the ocean?"

"It is the largest body of water imaginable and it is made of salty water," the wise old pheasant answered.

Timothy was now more confused than when he started asking the questions. He did not understand why the giants would bring the pheasants from the land of jade just to hunt and kill them. He also did not understand what was meant by the land of jade or the ocean, for that matter. He did know that the pheasant was not a willing alien. His kind had been brought across the ocean against their will.

Timothy had more questions than answers. He even wondered if his kind might not be aliens and he just did not know it. He felt sorry for the wise old pheasant, but he knew that Gerald was accurate in calling the wise old pheasant an alien.

Timothy went on, "Why do the crows hate you?"

"They believe we are aliens. They were here first, and they think we have come in to steal their food and take away their land."

"Is that true?" Timothy asked.

"No! *We only take what we need and nothing more, and who knows, if the giants weren't trying to kill us, they might focus on the crows and try to kill them. Also, Timothy, this is our home now; we would not even know how to go back to our native land. We certainly cannot fly well enough to fly across the ocean,"* the wise old pheasant responded.

He then exploded into flight, and Timothy watched as the big bird flew swiftly away in a straight line.

Can you find the other hidden pheasant?

Timothy was always amazed at how well and fast the pheasant could fly, but he did realize that Gerald was better at flying than the wise old pheasant.

Timothy understood a little better what the word alien meant, but he also realized that what that word meant in the hatred between the crows and the pheasants was very difficult to fathom.  He felt such concern for his friend, the wise old pheasant, that he decided to try to find out where the land of jade was on the other side of the ocean.  He also thought that if he could possibly understand the giants better, maybe he could understand how he might be able to end the war between the crows and the pheasants.  And above all, a field mouse is a curious animal, and Timothy's curiosity about the subject of aliens had been piqued to the maximum.  *He became a mouse on a mission of discovery and change!*

# Disking

Timothy was spending a lot more time in the hedgerow.  The fallow field had turned into a jumbled-up field of dirt clods and broken plants.  He could still forage for plant food and insects in the open field, but he was very exposed in the deeply plowed field to predators, so he decided that it would be best if most of the time, he remained hidden in the hedgerow.

What is the name of the flying predator?  Can you find the hidden field mouse?

Because the ripping plow had dug so deeply in the earth, the field now had the scent of plants, water, mud, and sweet earth.  Soon the giants disked the jumbled-up field with a disking plow.  The disking plow broke up the clods into small, fine soil, and after repeated disking, the field was level and very uniform in appearance and odor.  As soon as the disking was completed the farmhouse stood out at the far end of the field. Timothy was more curious than ever about the giants, so he started to watch the farmhouse. He would steal away under the yard fence to a place in the sweet pea thicket, and there he would wait and watch the farmyard and giants.

Soon Timothy learned many things about the giants that lived in the farmhouse. The little farm girl Lucina, was always outside playing with the farm animals or riding her bicycle. The boy, Will, would often come out to play fetch with the golden retriever, Sunny.

Timothy took special note of the golden retriever's love of chasing the ball.

The dog seemed to lose track of everything else and only paid attention to chasing the ball.

The little blonde girl, Lucina, fascinated Timothy. She seemed to love all animals, and all animals seemed to feel comfortable around her. Timothy even saw a little hummingbird land on her shoulder and sit there. In his dreams and also in waking life Lucina had tried to talk to him. He could not understand her, but the fact that she was trying to talk to him made him wonder what she might be trying to tell him. He had many questions about the giants, and Timothy wondered if maybe Lucina could answer some of those questions if she could talk to him. He remembered what his mother had said about his green piece of jade, and he wondered if, in Lucina's burrow, he might make some discoveries that could answer some of his questions. He was especially interested in where the piece of jade came from because of what the wise old pheasant had told him about the land of origin for his kind being the *land of jade.*

Timothy watched Lucina come and go in and out of her house, and he decided that she must have her burrow inside the farmhouse. He wanted to visit her burrow because he had come to believe that inside her burrow, he might find some answers to the riddle of the jade and the original home of the wise old pheasant. He also wanted to understand this giant better because maybe she could help him understand the ways of the giants.

Timothy was able to plan a way to get inside the farmhouse and find Lucina's burrow because from his vantage point in the sweet pea thicket, he could easily see the farmhouse door and the way that the family and animals entered and left the farmhouse.

Timothy decided that during the midday, when both the dog Sunny and Patches the cat were usually asleep, he would try to get in the house through the main door which was usually a little bit ajar. But getting into the house was only part of his problem in visiting Lucina's burrow. He had to escape safely back to his burrow as well. Because the field was so open after disking, he felt he should wait for the cover of some mature plants before trying to investigate Lucina's burrow. Otherwise, he would never be able to escape a pursuing dog, cat, or an open field predator like a fox or red-tailed hawk.

# Fertilizing

Shortly after the disking tractors had made the open field level and finely broken up, Timothy saw the tractor return, pulling a manure spreader that evenly spread manure over the top of the newly disked field. Timothy could smell that the manure was a mixture of cow, horse, pig and chicken poop. At this point in time, Timothy started to remain more in the hedgerow.  He was not at all fond of the smell of poop.

It was not long until the farmers returned with their tractor and worked the top layer of manure into the under layers of soil.  When it rained, the soil mixed with the manure and became much richer in nitrogen and minerals that would feed new plants.  It also smelled much better.  Timothy could tell that the farmers were preparing the earth to nourish the new plants, and he began to get excited about the coming germination and new plant life, but Timothy could tell that the wise old pheasant was right; the cotton field was going to be very different from the other farm fields he had lived in.

Timothy missed his mom.  He wondered what happened to her and why he never saw her again.  He also wondered about what she seemed to be hiding.  He had searched in the hedgerow for her burrow.  He asked the wise old pheasant if he knew where her burrow was, and the wise old pheasant told him that he did not know his mother from other field mice.

Timothy was very lonely. He did not know how to find his mother, and he missed Cindy mouse. He felt comforted by his piece of jade in his burrow because it reminded him of Cindy mouse and his mouslings. He curled up and went to sleep with his little mouse head resting on his green jade cross.

Timothy began to dream. He was looking out across the open disked field and the farmhouse. He watched the little blonde girl go in the house. He waited to see if she would come out again. He waited for a long time, and nobody came out of the house. He was hoping to see something that would tell him more about the giants and maybe about the little blonde girl. Then he saw a different kind of giant come out of the house.

Can you find what is written in the shaman's headband?

The shaman was tall with jet black hair; he did not have extra layers of skin made of cotton.  Instead he had animal skin around his waist.  There were *black crow feathers in his hair* held by a beaded headband. The shaman walked straight toward Timothy as if he knew exactly where Timothy was hidden in the hedgerow.  He seemed to be coming out of the farmhouse to meet with Timothy.  Timothy thought of fleeing, but for some reason he was not afraid of this giant.  This giant was very different from the other giants that Timothy had seen.  There was a special aura about him.  He seemed to come from another place and another time.  Timothy waited.  When the shaman was very close he said, "I salute you Timothy, you are a mouse with a purpose."

*Timothy was shocked that he understood the shaman perfectly. He was also shocked by the respect that the shaman had for him.*

Timothy said to the shaman with the crow feathers in his hair, "How can I understand you, and why do you show me, a field mouse, such respect?"

"I have learned all of the Great Spirit's creatures deserve honor and respect, especially the field mouse because there are few creatures that are as quick to make decisions and as fast to escape danger.  Because I have become a servant of wild nature, I have been granted the ability to communicate with the field mouse," the shaman answered.

The shaman held his hand toward Timothy with his palm upward and with his fingers closed on his palm.  *Then he opened his fingers, and in his palm was Timothy's mother.*

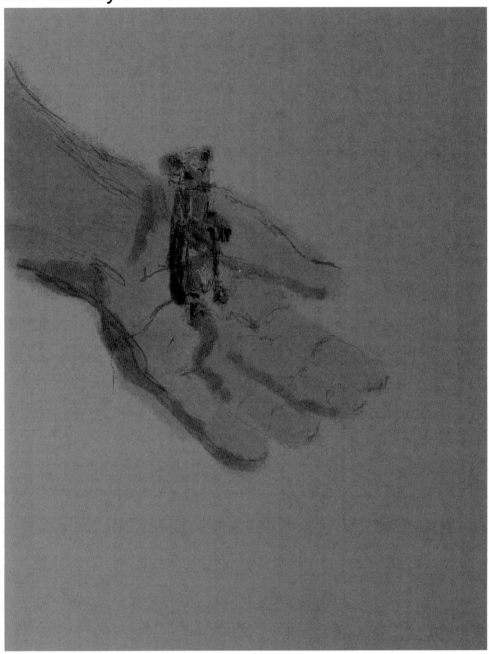

Timothy stared in amazement at his mother. She looked frightened. She spoke, "Timothy, I was hungry. After the giants ripped the field, I could not find enough food to produce milk for my mouseling. I went into the industrial farm. I found little pouches with delicious little bits of food in them. I thought that the giants were trying to take care of me. After I ate the food from the little pouches, I became very sick. I could no longer take care of my mouseling. *You must find her or she will die.*"

Timothy was frantic! He asked his mom, "Where is she?"

The giant closed his palm, turned around, and walked back toward the farmhouse. Timothy ran after him yelling, "Where is she?" "Where is she?" But the shaman with the crow feathers in his hair did not turn or answer he just kept walking away. When he walked back into the farm house Timothy woke up.

Timothy knew now what his mother had kept from him. *He also knew that out there somewhere in the field, he had a sister, and if he didn't find her soon, she would die!*

# Listing Up the Rows

Timothy realized that his sister could not be out in the area being prepared to grow cotton.  He knew that his mother's burrow had to be somewhere out of the path of the tractors, but where?  Soon a tractor returned to list up the rows for planting by cutting deep furrows.  The tractor pulled a furrowing plow that made eight very deep furrows at equal distances apart.  Now the field was a field of very symmetrical hills and valleys, and Timothy knew that soon the water would flow between those mounds of fresh dirt.  Timothy was at a loss to figure out how to find his mother's burrow in time to save his little sister.

Timothy went to find the wise old pheasant.  The wise old pheasant was not to be found.  Then Timothy ran in patterns up and down the hedgerow hoping to find a scent of his mother or the mouseling.  He went looking in the bushes and thick plants in the hedgerow.

He became so frantic that he went out into the mounded field and from the top of a mound yelled out, "GERALD!" In the world of field mouse behavior, this desperate act was indeed not well thought out. With just about every animal that eats other animals willing to kill a field mouse for food, Timothy was not acting at all wisely. He was a desperate mouse who put himself in an unsafe situation. Fortunately, Gerald heard his mouse scream and flew to his aid.

When Gerald arrived, Timothy was not at all sure that it was Gerald. He realized that he had put himself in a bad position, but he had faith, and I guess we could say that although without wings to catch him like the birds could, Timothy had become used to taking leaps of faith when he became desperate or adventuresome.

Gerald landed in front of Timothy. He tilted his head to the right, then to the left, and then he touched his beak to the ground in front of Timothy. "What's wrong, Timothy?" Gerald asked.

"I had a dream. I saw a man wearing your feathers in his hair. He opened his hand, and I saw my mother. She told me that she had eaten food that made her sick, and she could not take care of my sister.  *Gerald, I have a mouseling sister, and I cannot find her.  If I don't find her soon, she will die!"*

"I have to tell you, Timothy, crows cannot be trusted when it comes to mouselings.  I would like to help you find this mouseling, but I cannot ask other crows about her, or I will put her at risk.  The giant with my kind's feathers in his hair is someone that I have heard of, and he would not have helped you if it was not very important for you to find this mouseling.  All that I can do is to get you out of this field before a predator ends your search for you."

With that, Timothy turned his side to Gerald and the big black bird picked him up and flew him to the hedgerow. When Gerald let Timothy go, at the hedgerow, he said to him, "Timothy, I would see what the quail know. They spend a great deal of time foraging in unusual places. Sometimes they will help if asked properly."

"How do I ask them properly, Gerald?" Timothy inquired.

"You must say that you are a mouse with a purpose, and Gerald the crow has sent you."

Timothy set out forthwith to find quail. It did not take him long. For, as fortune would have it, a covey of quail were close by in the hedgerow. Timothy knew that the quail would only speak in turns, so he hoped to hear from one of them first. He went up close to them and waited for one to speak.

"Hello," said the first quail.

"Who," said the second quail.

"Are," said the third quail.

"You?" said the fourth quail.

Timothy answered, "I am Timothy the mouse with a purpose, and I have been sent by Gerald."

With that, all of the quail exploded into flight and left Timothy standing, confused and alone. His first thought was, "Oh well, that did not work." Or at least it seemed that way until he heard another quail voice.

The hedgerow is the wild area of the farm. Animals meet there and find refuge. Because of the diversity of habitat, there are many sources of food for wild animals. How many things can you find in hedgerow that Timothy or the trailer quail can eat?

"I am the trailer quail. I always stay behind. I study what happens next so that I can report to the covey, and because I must be alone after they leave, to observe and report to my covey, I can speak as an individual. My reports make it so that our covey can be safer by learning from what happens after they leave."

"You must know a lot," Timothy said.

"I have learned many things by staying after the others have left, and now I have learned about you."

"There is more to learn about me," Timothy said.

"What is your mystery that I may report?" asked the trailer quail.

"I am trying desperately to find a mouseling that was left by my mother.  The mother mouse can no longer take care of her, and she is too young to take care of herself."

"Is she black?" asked the trailer quail.

"I do not know, but in a dream, I chased a black mouse," Timothy said.

"There is a black mouseling all alone where the water comes out, and she will soon die when the canal fills with water.  And now I must go and report what you are doing."  With that, her small but powerful wings exploded into flight as she flew to give her report.

Timothy was grateful for the help of the trailer quail, but he still did not know where his mouseling sister was. He asked himself, "Where does the water come out?"

He thought to himself, "Water comes out of the clouds in the sky, but that would mean that his sister could be anywhere. Water can come from the pipes that irrigate, but there were so many of them."

Then Timothy had an idea. He would try to think like his mother. Where would he put a mouseling if he were her? The only clue he had to go on was what the trailer quail had told him about the place where the water came out, but just then he remembered she had said something else. Not only did he say that the mouseling was where the water came out, but he also said, "Soon she would die."

Timothy knew that now that the listing up of planting rows was done, soon the water would flow in the furrows to give the new plants plenty of moisture. He also knew, from the time he had played on the fantastic water machine in the wheat field, that the water would come from the irrigation canal and be piped down the furrows.

All of a sudden, Timothy put what the trailer quail had said together. Realizing that soon the irrigation canal would fill with water for the furrows, *his sister must be in the irrigation canal where the fill water comes out.*

Just then Timothy heard the powerful irrigation pump kick on.  He ran as fast as he could to where the water was rushing out to fill the irrigation canal.

The noise was deafening; the water spray was shooting everywhere.   Under the huge irrigation pipe, he could see where his mother had placed twigs and grass to conceal the burrow's entrance.

Can you find the mouseling hidden in her mother's burrow?

Timothy remembered his mad dash to his mother's burrow during the great flood and how he thought that he was too late. He had to be faster this time if he was to save his sister!

He jumped to a narrow ledge of dirt just before the entrance to the burrow. It was already muddy and his feet slipped as he hurried underneath the huge water pipe. He frantically pushed aside the twigs and grass to reveal the burrow opening. He could smell his mother's scent inside the burrow. He knew that he had found her burrow, but where was his sister?

It was very dark inside the burrow, and he could not see a mouseling, but he could smell the scent of a mouseling. Why couldn't he see her? Then he remembered, "You mean the black mouseling."

He followed his nose and found his black mouseling sister by scent and touch. He ran right into her soft furry side. She was trembling with fear and was so young.

"We have to get out of here," Timothy yelled at her.

"Oh, no I cannot go,

My mother told me so.

I must stay. I cannot play.

My mother will come for me today," she said in perfect rhyme.

Field mice are some of the fastest creatures on earth to adapt.  They have to be because they are prey to so many animals and their size is so small; if they do not adapt quickly to new situations, they would never be able to stay ahead of other creatures enough to survive.

With his sister, Timothy was looking at a whole new world.  She was young and helpless.  She did not know him.  She was an unusual color for a field mouse, and if all of that wasn't enough, she was a poetical mouse.  And he had about ten seconds to convince her to leave the burrow before she would drown.

"Your mother and my mother, too,

Sent me to save you.

The water is coming fast.

In your burrow you will not last.

Your life can end here way too fast

Because your burrow soon will flood with a terrible blast."

Timothy spoke to his little sister in rhyme.  He had quickly adapted to her form of speech so that she could understand and hopefully accept what he had to say.

It worked, she turned toward the opening to the burrow and fled. Timothy's sister ran past Timothy and out of the burrow ahead of him.  *She was faster than Timothy!*

# Deep Irrigation

When the mice were safely out of the irrigation ditch, they both looked back.  They saw the entrance to the burrow go completely under the swirling muddy water.

"Brother, you saved me.

In your debt, I will always be."

Now that his sister was in the light, Timothy could see that she was young but quite strong and healthy.  He also thought that she was a very beautiful black mouse.

"What is your name?" Timothy asked.

"My mother named me Timothina."

She said,

"I was meant to be poetical.

So, that I could more than practical.

I was gifted with speed

In word and deed.

My color is rare,

With no other mouse, would I compare.

I must be fast and help my brother

Because he is a mouse of purpose unlike any other.

Now that you have found me,

Are you indeed the mouse of purpose named Timothy?"

Timothy was amazed by his sister.  *What a mouse, black in color, faster than any mouse he had known, and poetical!*

As impressed as Timothy was by his sister, he knew she was still a mouseling and needed a great deal of support from him. He also knew that they were not out of danger.

"Timothina, follow me. I will lead you to your new burrow," Timothy said.

Timothina responded,

"I miss my mother,

but now I have a brother."

And with that, she followed Timothy as he led her through the deeper grass and weeds in the hedgerow to his burrow in the blackberry bush. When Timothina saw the wonderful piece of jade with the little green cross inside Timothy's burrow, she stopped short.  She tried to sniff it.  Then she cautiously approached it.  She walked around it sideways never taking her eyes off of it.  It was almost as if she expected it to jump out and get her.

Timothy laughed, "It won't hurt you, Timothina.  It is my treasure.  It makes me feel better when I am alone, and it helps me to dream when I am asleep."

Finally, after some minutes, Timothina seemed to accept the piece of jade.  In fact she laid down and put her head on it.  Then she got up and said,

"Timothy, what should I do?

I am hungry,

and everything here is new.

My stomach is angry."

Timothy responded, "Follow me we will forage together. I will watch for predators while you look for tender plants and insects.  We must stay close together so that we can forage and watch as a team. When you have eaten your stomach will not be angry."

Timothy took Timothina along the side of the irrigation ditch where they easily found enough insects to eat because the insects were fleeing the rapidly rising water.

When night fell, they returned to their burrow. Timothina was no longer as frightened by the new surroundings and she curled up next to Timothy. Soon both mice were fast asleep with both of their little heads pressed against the green cross.

Can you find the important hidden word in the dirt of the mouse burrow?

Timothy soon was dreaming. Again he was at the edge of the meadow, watching the farmhouse, and again, the shaman with the black feathers in his hair came walking toward him. When the shaman was close, he opened his hand and there was his mother. "Timothy," she said softly, "you have found Timothina. Thank you, I will worry no more. I must go now.  I will wait for you on the other side of the portal."

Timothy quickly asked, "What portal Mother?"  But the giant closed his hand and walked away before his mother could answer.  Timothy woke up with a start, but there, next to him in the moonlight was his beautiful black sister.  He looked at the way the moonlight glistened on her coat, and for the first time in a long time, he did not feel all alone.  He put his head back down and fell asleep, dreaming of playing with his sister in a wonderful fallow field.

# Pre-planting Irrigation

Timothy and Timothina woke up when it was still dark, and they were surprised to find the giants were working along the hedgerow.  They were placing siphon pipes from the irrigation canal to the individual furrows.   And with the moon still up, it was easy to see that the field was filling with water.

Can you see the fish swimming in the filled irrigation ditch?

Timothy remembered what the wise old pheasant had said, that the ripping was done so that the irrigation water would sink in deep, and he realized that the giants were going to put a lot of water on the field for that deep irrigation. Timothina and Timothy watched from the safety of their hedgerow as the field filled with water. Eventually, only the bare tops of the listed up furrows could be seen above the water.  There were plenty of insects to eat because they were fleeing the flooded field.  Timothy worked hard to teach his sister how to be safe and forage for herself.  Sometimes, when he felt she would be safer in their burrow, he had her stay there, and he brought her plants, flowers and fruit to eat.

Timothina, like all mouselings, grew fast and in a very short time, she was spending more and more time with Timothy.  Every day Timothy taught Timothina  the skills necessary to be a successful field mouse.  Timothy learned very quickly that he could depend on Timothina to watch for predators and to be helpful in any way that she could.

He explained to her what their mother had said about his piece of jade.  He told her that he wanted to find out where it came from and how he might return it.  He also explained to her about his interest in finding out more about what it meant to be an alien and what made Gerald dislike the wise old pheasant because he was an alien.

Timothina would learn the lessons of the day, and then sometimes, she would sum things up with poetry.  Timothy also came to realize that the poems of Timothina could contain much more information than a normal spoken sentence. He learned to listen to her poems for layers of meaning. There could be new ways of looking at things, cautions, and even glimpses of the future in her poetical language.

"My brother Timothy is thinking of the farmhouse.

He wants to know what could be in there.

He is one curious mouse.

But if he goes into the house, he must beware.

The giants keep the house,

And Patches the cat and Sunny the dog are there.

I must help my brother with my speed.

My help he will surely need," thus Timothina spoke.

Timothy listened carefully and replied, "Timothina, we will watch the house together. You can help me when I try. If we are not successful, I am afraid I will fail in my purpose. I want to learn more about the land of jade, where the giant with the crow feathers came from and the little blonde girl."

Timothy and Timothina studied the house together trying to figure out how to safely get into the house and even more importantly, how to get out. Timothy noticed that at about the same time every day, the cat and dog fell asleep, and the giants all seemed to be out of the house. Even better was the fact that the door to the house was sometimes left ajar with just enough space for two field mice to enter.

With the field at this time being mostly mud and bare mounds of dirt, the garden by the house with the rich variety of edible plants looked very tempting to the mice as well. Timothy and Timothina decided to try to get to the garden in order to forage and test the safety of entering the farmyard.

When the dog and cat had fallen asleep, the two field mice slipped under the wooden fence and went through the sweet peas to the garden. There they nibbled on the carrot and radish tops.

Bees are pollinating the flowers in the garden.  Can you find the two bumblebees?

They also found insects to eat.  When they were finished, they stealthily slipped out the same way that they went in.  Both the cat and the dog slept through the whole incursion.

With the success of foraging in the garden, the mice realized with the correct timing, they could probably enter the house.  Timothy was ready to give it a try, but first he thought that he should talk to the wise old pheasant because the wise old pheasant always seemed to know something that he had failed to think of.

Timothy found the wise old pheasant near his normal roost. "Hello, wise old pheasant. I would like to talk to you about something that I have been planning," Timothy said.

"Tlot, tlot,tlot, but who is the black mouseling with you?" the wise old pheasant answered.

"That is my sister Timothina; she is a poetical mouseling of rare color who can run like the wind," Timothy replied.

"Wise old pheasant, I have heard from Timothy about you.

I must help my brother so that one mouse can be two," Timothina said, without being asked.

Tlot, tlot, tlot the wise old pheasant stood on his toes and flapped his wings.

"What a treat of a mouse are you.

And so very fast, too," the wise old pheasant responded poetically.

"What is your query, Timothy?" the wise old pheasant asked.

"I plan to go into the giant's burrow because I want to find out more about the land of jade where the giants captured your ancestors.  I am interested in the little blonde girl who keeps trying to talk to me and I want to find out where the shaman who brought my mother to me in his hand comes from. *There are many mysteries in that big giant burrow and I want to solve some of them!*"

"You are indeed a curious field mouse, and you are to be praised for your curiosity; however, curiosity can be a dangerous thing.  The giant's world is very different from ours.  They cannot see the things that we see, and they are very slow.  If you learn something from them you must take it with you and flee very quickly.  They do not belong to our wild world.  They cannot understand wild animals," the wise old pheasant said.

"What does it mean to be a wild animal?" Timothy asked the wise old pheasant.

"A wild animal is free, Timothy.  A wild animal is nurtured by Mother Earth and stays apart from the giants. They all have something hidden inside of them that keeps them from being wild. When you and Timothina leave the natural part of the farm and enter the giant's world you both will be in grave danger.  You must not eat or drink anything in the house. What you take can only be feelings and memories so that you can learn from them. Anything else will put you in grave danger. And with that, the wise old pheasant exploded in flight and left the two mice to think about what he had said.

Timothy was glad that he talked to the wise old pheasant.  He would have never thought of leaving good food untouched, and sometimes he liked to steal a drink if water was available.  He also remembered what his mother had said about the piece of jade, "That he should return it because it was a part of the world of the giants."

The field was full of irrigation water.  The tops of the furrows were just barely visible above the water. The giants had kept the irrigation water on the field for a greater length of time than Timothy had ever seen.  In fact, with the cotton field, everything seemed to be exaggerated.  The ripper plowed deeper, and now the water stood longer and sank deeper into the ground.

The mice waited for their chance.  The farmhouse door was slightly ajar. Patches and Sunny were taking their nap. The two mice moved quickly through the grass at the edge of the farmhouse and under the wood fence; they hid in the sweet peas for awhile and then ran to the front door of the farmhouse and went in.

Once in the farmhouse, Timothy followed the scent of the little blonde girl.  He thought that if he could find her individual burrow, he would be able to learn more about the mysteries that held such a fascination for him.  He also hoped that by understanding the giants better, he could help the wild animals that were his friends.  Where did the giant with the crow feathers in his hair come from? What was the little blonde girl trying to tell him?

Down the hall of the farmhouse and into Lucina's bedroom they went.  Timothina froze in front of

Lucina's dreamcatcher.

Find the hidden word in the dreamcatcher.

There she saw the black crow feathers hanging down from the bottom of the dreamcatcher. She could also see the black wolf with the yellow eyes.

She said to Timothy, "Brother dear, I have found where the giant with the crow feathers comes from, here."

Timothy looked up at the dreamcatcher and said, "Yes, Timothina, you are correct, I see the feathers of the crow and the black predator of my dreams. And now I want to find out more about this giant and why she is so different from the other giants."

Timothy ran and jumped onto Lucina's bed. Then he scurried across and jumped onto her large green teddy bear. He was able to climb the teddy bear because of the long fur, and then when he was safely on top of the large teddy bear's head, he could see Lucina's shelf holding her altar.

Look for the teddy bear's name.

He was amazed at the sight of Mother Mary holding her baby Jesus surrounded by the jade tigers and the smiling Buddha.  He wanted to get on the shelf of wondrous statues but he could not figure out how to do it.

He was looking at the shelf in wonder when he saw something he could hardly believe.  There on the shelf just behind one of the jade tigers was his sister!

"How did you get up there, Timothina?" Timothy asked.

"I asked the giant with the crow feathers in his hair
How do I get myself up there?

He told me to look at the feathers of the crow

 And to those feathers, I must go.

When I was hanging from the feather of the crow,

I started to swing, to and fro.

It was when I saw the jade tiger that I let go.

I few through the air and landed here just so."

Timothy followed his sister's lead, and by swinging
from the feathers at the bottom of the dreamcatcher
and letting go at just the right time, he was able to fly
to the altar shelf. There he saw the collection of
jade.

He realized he had found a collection of things that
belonged to the land of jade that existed on the other
side on the ocean.  He also knew that his precious
piece of jade had belonged to the little blonde girl
and was part of this collection.  He understood why
his mother had told him that the green jade cross did
not belong to him.  As he walked around the magical
world created on Lucina's altar shelf, he realized

more about what it meant to be an alien.  This world of jade that was collected to represent where the wise old pheasant's ancestors came from, was very different indeed from the farm where Timothy and Timothina lived.  This small microcosm of the land over the sea was enough to help Timothy realize that to be from such a place would cause the wise old pheasant's kind to be very different and unique and maybe difficult to understand.  He remembered what the wise old pheasant had said, "They all have something hidden in them that keeps them from being wild."

Timothy had found what he had come for.  He told his sister, "Timothina, we must flee as fast as can be.  This giant's burrow is not a proper place for us!"

Getting on the altar shelf had been one thing but getting off was quite another.  With the crow feathers hanging limply at the bottom of the dreamcatcher they could not be reached.  The bed seemed too far to jump to, and just then the mice heard the footfalls of a giant coming down the hall. Timothy knew those steps; they were of the little blonde girl.  He did not know what to do.  He did not know how to protect

Timothina; he suddenly felt very alone and afraid. The only thing that made him feel better was the fact that he knew it was the little blonde girl who seemed so different from the other giants and also so kind. He also knew she was the same little girl who had tried to talk to him in the cornfield and also in his dreams. He called out to Timothina to try to hide. They were too late. It was as if she knew they were there on her altar shelf. The footfalls suddenly became very rapid. She was running. Both mice instinctively froze in place.

Lucina ran into her room and turned so that she was looking right at her altar shelf.

She could hardly believe her eyes. There, to the right of her jade tiger on the left side of smiling

Buddha, was a pure black mouse looking at her. On the other side of the Mother Mary, on the left side of her jade tiger, was a brown mouse with some white fur that had grown in where the mouse had been scratched.

Lucina spoke so softly, "I had a feeling I would find you here and I was right! Aren't you two a pair of beautiful mice? I won't hurt you, but you need to return to the field. I know you are wild, and you should not be here. You must have come on some kind of a special mission, and I can both understand and respect that. If you will climb onto my hands, I will return you to the field."

It was then that Timothy saw it. In her hair was one black crow feather. When Lucina held out her hands with the palms up, Timothy remembered his dream, and even though he could not understand her sounds, he understood completely the gesture of the outstretched hands palms up. He told Timothina, "We must climb onto her outstretched palms because in a strange way, she understands us and why we are here."

Timothina said,

"I can see the crow's feather in her hair,

And as you say, dear brother, I will go there."

No one could ever know or believe the powerful magic that transpired in Lucina's bedroom as two mice willingly walked from beside the jade tigers into her waiting palms.

Lucina walked slowly down the hall

past the kitchen and dining room to the front door of the farmhouse.  As soon as she was outside of the farmhouse, she knelt down and gently placed her hands on the ground with her palms up.  Timothy and Timothina ran from her hands for the fence and the open, flooded field.

Sunny slept through the whole thing, but Patches woke just in time to see the mice go under the fence. Lucina yelled, "No, Patches!" But of course Patches, paid no mind and ran around the fence and through the open gate, hoping to catch them on the other side.

With the field nearly full of water and paths for animals to follow restricted, Strand the fox was able to pick up the mouse scent.  He recognized the scent of the magical mouse, but there was also a new scent.  The magical mouse was in the company of a younger mouse.  He remembered how the older mouse had confused him and caused him to fail in catching the younger Timothy.  He also remembered how he had failed when he tried to have the two-mouse meal.  He felt good about this combination of mice that he was following. He was not going to be tricked or make the same mistakes. He would focus on catching and eating only the magical mouse! But where were these mice going? Surely they were not going to the farmhouse. But as he followed the scent he was being drawn closer and closer to the farmhouse. Soon he was in a clump of grass very nearly at the edge of the farmhouse. They must have gone in. Strand was a fox in the true sense of the word. He was very intelligent! He found a place to hide and wait. He was also very patient, like all predators. While he was waiting, he was dreaming of the power he would gain by eating the magical mouse. He also was intelligent enough to be curious as to why the magical mouse had gone into the land of the giants. Was he on a mission of magic? Could he somehow obtain more magic inside the world of the giants? And if he did obtain more magic from the giants, would that make him even more powerful and magical when he ate the magical mouse?

You can imagine how the last thought was re-enforced when Strand, to his disbelieving eyes, saw the little blonde girl come out of the house ceremoniously supporting two mice in the palms of her hands, and when she knelt down and they both fled, he believed he was witnessing some kind of magical ceremony. He watched them run for the fence, and he waited patiently for them to appear on his side of the fence that separated his wild world from the world of the giants. He waited with great anticipation. His mouth began to water at the thought of the delicious mouse meal that was about to confer upon him magical powers that would redefine his position. He would become the greatest of all red foxes. He would become Strand the magical one!

When the mice came under the fence, Strand was totally focused; he was not about to let the black mouse distract him, and besides she was younger and faster than the brown mouse anyway. So, he had no trouble trying for the older Timothy because this was in accordance with the unwritten code of predation.

I guess you could say at this juncture that Strand was correct in a way about the magical mouse theory. Timothy, and now Timothina, were beginning to live in a dream life of purpose. They had slipped into a world that indeed was quite magical, and Strand the fox, for all of his faults, must be acknowledged as the first among wild animals to recognize Timothy as a magical mouse. Of course he was very foolish to think that he could gain extra magical power by eating Timothy, but then again, power-hungry foxes are not always the brightest of animals on the farm. *As is the case with all power-crazed animals, their passion for power clouds their judgment!*

In the end two very fast predators, Patches the cat and Strand the fox, collided. They both had tunnel vision! They were so focused on their prey they were oblivious of each other until it was too late.

Timothina was so fast, and at the same time, concerned for Timothy that when she looked back she saw a sight that she would never forget. It was a blur of white and black fur all mixed up with the reddish coat of the fox.

Find what is written in the clouds.

And the sounds, well, I don't suppose you can imagine a mouse smile, but if you can, I would like you to imagine Timothina grinning from ear to ear at the hissing and barking that went on as these two predators (one from the wild side of the fence and one from the tame side of the fence) mixed it up and, for a short time, tried to best one another in combat. All the while, Timothy made his escape.

Soon Patches and Strand realized that this combat was going nowhere, and they quickly disentangled themselves and returned to their proper side of the fence, both mentally and physically. Strand had some scratches that he would spend days licking in order to get them to heal, and Patches was on her way to the veterinarian's office to be treated for fox bites. Oh, and I should add that when Lucina saw Patches come back bloodied up with fox bites and *no mouse,* she probably shouldn't have been glad, but she was.

Needless to say, Strand became ever more convinced of the magical power of Timothy and even though he wanted to try again to gain that power, he was beginning to have  both a greater respect for the magical mouse and greater doubts about his ability to achieve Timothy's special magical power for himself. He was beginning to think that maybe just maybe, the magical mouse was too powerful to mess with, but he wasn't ready to give up quite yet!

Safely back in the burrow, Timothy was surprised to find that Timothina was not angry with him. In fact she told Timothy,

"I saw the giant's house on the inside

And many secrets the giant did confide.

The giant was friendly and fair.

She treated us with understanding when we were there."

Timothy replied, "Timothina, I now know more about my piece of jade, about the land of jade, and also where the shaman in my dreams came from.  The giant girl is really different from the other giants and for the first time, I understood her when she held out her hands with the palms up."

Timothy was even more interested in the girl and her farmhouse, and now he had many questions.  He wondered how the girl knew they were in her room and why she treated them with such kindness.  How did she know about their mission?

He knew that his piece of jade belonged to her and she had lost it in the field.  He also knew that he had to try to return the piece of jade to her even though he would miss it very much.  He understood that he would have to pay more attention to the girl in order to figure out how to return her piece of jade.  By entering the farmhouse, Timothy had become more involved with Lucina, and he wondered if she was an important part of what the wise old pheasant and others had described as his "purpose."

The days passed, and the giants stopped irrigating the field because the deep irrigation was completed. Timothina and Timothy remained in the hedgerow close to their burrow as the field dried. The foraging was easy because of the abundance of water, the vegetation was lush, and there were many insects. The field mice avoided the field because as the earth dried, it became very smooth and hard so that a field mouse would be easily seen by a predator. However, the field was also warmer than the hedgerow, so Timothy and Timothina would run out in the furrows at night and lay absolutely still to feel the warmth of the soil against their bellies.

# Mulching

Lucina was amazed by how accurate her dream had been. She had seen an Indian shaman with a crow feathers in his hair. He had told her that she should look for a brown and black mouse on her altar shelf.

He had explained how, when she found them, she was to hold her hands outstretched, palms up, and when they were in her hands, how she was to take them back to the wild where they came from.

It was late and she had been reading for a long time. She was so excited she believed that she would never go to sleep. She was thinking about the field mice when she fell asleep and started to dream. This time she was outside of her house in the hedgerow when she saw the shaman approach. He said, "Lucina you did well to return the mice to the wild, thank you."

Lucina asked, "Who were they?"

The shaman answered, "Timothy and Timothina, two very important field mice."

Lucina asked, "Why are they so important?"

The shaman held his hand outstretched over the field and said, "The brown mouse named Timothy is my brother."

Lucina was very puzzled, "How can you have a mouse for a brother?"

The shaman did not answer; he just turned to walk away, but before he disappeared, she heard him say, "Look for the brown mouse."

Lucina woke with a start. She wasn't sure if she had been dreaming or awake. She decided she must have been dreaming. She read for a little while longer, then fell asleep. This time she did not wake up until it was time to get ready for school. She could not remember any of her dreams except the one with the Indian shaman in it.

In the morning, at breakfast, her father asked her if she would like to help him mulch the cotton field after school. She loved to help her dad with his tractor work, so she said very emphatically, "Yes!"

Timothy told Timothina, "The giants will soon do something because the ground is getting very dry again, but I cannot understand why they have not planted. Everything seems to be taking much more time in preparation for the cotton plants."

Timothina answered,

"When the change comes, it will be new for me.

I will look for the world of cotton to grow free.

Maybe cotton grows slow.

How little of cotton I know."

For some reason, when Timothina talked about the cotton growing free, Timothy thought that maybe the cotton would grow for a longer time without the giants doing anything to it. In this way her poetical phrasing helped Timothy to understand why the cotton field was taking so long to prepare. Timothy was beginning to believe that the best thing that ever happened to him was to find his wonderful black poetical sister mouse.

Timothy looked out and saw the tractor. It was pulling a trailer that evenly spread the cotton mulch. The cotton mulch smelled very different to Timothy. He had never smelled such plant silage before. He thought that it was strange that the giants had chosen to spread silage from a plant that he had never known to grow in his field. He wondered why and decided that when the field was mulched, he was going to investigate this new type of silage.

Then he saw something that made his little mouse heart pump with excitement. On the tractor next to the older giant was the blonde girl.

What is written on Lucina's father's cap?

This was his chance to return the piece of jade, but he didn't have much time.  He had to act fast.

He told Timothina to wait in the blackberry bush because he was going to try to return the green jade cross to the girl and he would be exposed to predators.  He ran as fast as he could to the burrow.

He picked up the piece of jade and hopped like a kangaroo toward the open field and the tractor.

He realized, after going a short distance, that he could not make it out in front of the tractor in time with the piece of jade by hopping. He needed help and he needed it fast.

He let out his loud squeak for Gerald. Gerald was very fond of watching the giants, and he had them all named. The little girl he called Lucy because he had heard her father call her name. He had grown close to Lucina because she paid a great deal of attention to the wild animals on the farm and had actually learned to communicate with him to a certain extent.

Gerald was flying over the field watching the giants mulch the future cotton field when he heard Timothy. He swooped down and landed next to him. "Timothy, why did you call?" Gerald asked.

"I need to return my piece of jade to the girl giant on the tractor with her father. I need to get in front of the tractor with this piece of jade fast!" Timothy responded.

Gerald told Timothy to hold onto his piece of jade. Then he jumped and picked up Timothy.

On the tractor with her father, Lucina, who always watched and tried to make friends with the animals on the farm, did not fail to notice the large crow at the edge of the field. She thought maybe that crow was Gerald.

Gerald was the name she had given to a crow whom she had befriended. He had taught her how to "count crow" as she called it. She had learned from Gerald how to greet with a single caw. How two caws meant to watch out for danger. Three caws meant that she should not worry because everything she was concerned about would work out fine. Four meant that something very important was complete. Five caws meant that Gerald the crow was very happy. And Gerald gave seven caws when he wanted her to join with him in celebrating the wonderful world of nature.

She decided the crow was not Gerald as soon as she saw him jump up and grab a mouse, because she had never seen Gerald eat anything but plant food. She watched as the crow flew out in front of the tractor with the prey animal in its talons.

To say she was surprised by what happened next would be an understatement. First, she heard the crow caw four times, which made her wonder if indeed the crow might not be Gerald. Then the crow flew to a place a little ways in front of the tractor, hovered briefly close to the ground and dropped the mouse!

She yelled, "Daddy, please stop the tractor!" Her father stopped the tractor, and Lucina made a mad dash to rescue the poor mouse. Again she was very surprised because the mouse waited until she was close enough to see by the white lines on its head, that it was the same brown mouse who had visited her room. Then he took off running as if nothing unusual had ever happened and he was just a wild field mouse running away from her.

She was suspicious of this whole turn of events. She thought of the four caws and remembered her dream and the instructions given by the Indian shaman, "To watch for the brown mouse." What could all of this mean? She slowly walked to the place where the mouse had landed when the crow (who by now she believed was indeed "Gerald") had dropped the mouse.

She could hardly believe her eyes. There, on the ground where the mouse had been, was her lost piece of jade. She picked it up reverently. She turned it over and over in her little hand.

How could this be? Was she dreaming? Had the mouse actually found and returned her special green jade cross? She was amazed. She was too amazed to even think. She ran back toward the tractor, yelling at the top of her voice, "Daddy, Daddy, the crow and the mouse returned my jade cross!"

When she returned to the tractor, her father said, "Lucina let me see your piece of jade?" She gave her green jade cross to her father. He turned it over and over in his hand then gave it back to Lucina. After he had studied it for a long time, he said, "You should put this green jade cross in a very special place where you will always know where it is." Lucina assured her father that she would. She then jumped off of the tractor and ran back to the farmhouse where she placed her green jade cross by the bottom of the Mother Mary statue. She then raced back to her waiting father and Lucina and her father continued to fill the furrows with the special cotton mulch.

When Timothy returned to the hedgerow, he didn't know if the girl giant had found her piece of jade or not. When he had ran from the field, he did not look back until he reached the safety of the hedgerow. Lucina was already going back to the tractor. He heard her yell but he could not understand her.

Back in the blackberry bush burrow, Timothina was very glad to see him. She jumped up and down and ran in circles. She said,

"My brother has returned.

How much I have learned.

I saw the crow take him into the sky.

I must say that I thought it was goodbye.

How good a friend can a crow be?

I will just have to wait and see.

And perhaps, I now understand,

Why the girl lifted us to safety with her hand.

Could this be part of a plan?"

That night, when Timothy and Timothina curled up and went to sleep, they missed the green jade cross and the way its presence comforted them. *But Timothy was glad that he had done his best to fulfill his mother's wishes to return the piece of jade. By succeeding Timothy felt wilder and freer of the giants and their world. That night Timothina and*

*Timothy dreamt well; they both had powerful wild mouse dreams.*

Timothy dreamt of flying far away with Gerald, and Timothina dreamt of a beautiful pond with huge pond lilies and many different kinds of animals that lived around the edge of the pond.

# The Mulch Period

Usually after plowing, furrow building, and irrigation, the planting of the new plants was not far behind, but like everything else with the cotton field the cotton mulch just sat out there between the furrows for a long period of time while the field remained barren. The rains had started to fall, and Timothy and Timothina foraged primarily in the hedgerow.

It was at the time of year when the pretty lights decorated the farmhouse and in the window there was a beautifully decorated tree, that Timothy accidentally found out what was discouraging insects and new plant growth in the mulched field. Like all field mice in the cold of the night, Timothina and Timothy would go out into the field and press their bellies against the warm earth.  One especially cold clear night when the decorative lights and tree at the farmhouse were especially pretty,

Can you see what Lucina wrote on the fence?

Timothy decided to try to lay belly down on the cotton mulch just to see if cotton mulch could make him warm like the heat from the dark earth. After running out into the furrowed field, Timothy stretched out over a pile of damp, old, cotton plant mulch. He was very surprised because the cotton mulch wasn't warm.  It was HOT!

Can you see the heat coming off of the decomposing cotton mulch?

The decomposing cotton mulch was so hot that Timothy felt like his fur was on fire.  He jumped up and ran.  The whole field was very hot because of the decomposing cotton plants.  Timothy then understood why there were so few insects and plants on the surface.  The cotton silage was heating up the whole field to the point that insects and plants were discouraged from growing or outright killed by the heat. The giants were cleansing the field with the heat and decomposition of the cotton mulch.

The mulch had made the field more inhospitable to the wild animals on the farm because of the paucity of plants and insects able to endure the extreme heat. Among all of the wild animals negatively affected by the mulching period were the crows. There seemed to be fewer and fewer of the crows in or near the field.

It was in this strange atmosphere of decomposing cotton mulch that something happened to change the way the animals on the Fontana farm were relating to one another. One day when Timothy and Timothina were foraging in the hedgerow Gerald landed nearby. Timothina recognized him as the friendly crow, so she was not frightened. Timothy ran up to him and asked him, "Where are all of the crows?"

Gerald responded, "Timothy, there is something that I must talk to you about. Something terrible is happening to us."

"What has happened, Gerald?" Timothy responded.

"We are becoming sick, and some of us are dying, and I do not know why."

Immediately Timothy said, without thinking, "I will ask the wise old pheasant about this." Then he remembered how little Gerald thought of the wise old pheasant.

Gerald ruffled his feathers, but then he seemed to calm down. "Timothy, you know that we do not have any respect for those aliens!"

It took a lot of courage for Timothy to say what he said next, "Gerald, are you stealing the eggs of the pheasants?"

Gerald's feathers ruffled, and he did something that Timothy had never seen before. He jumped on one foot and then the other, and Timothy could tell he was very angry. When he stopped jumping up and down, he said, "Timothy, I would never steal any eggs. You know I do not eat anything but plant food."

"The wise old pheasant says that the crows steal the eggs of his kind."

What happened next really surprised both Timothy and Gerald. Timothina, who had quietly come closer to the two animals said,

"The crow does not lie.

The pheasant does not lie.

But something must be understood in the why.

For as things are, both will die."

Gerald became very calm and so did Timothy. Gerald walked slowly and deliberately to where Timothina was waiting. He tilted his head to the right, then to the left, and then he touched his peak the ground in front of Timothina.

"Black mouse, I see you have the gift of poetry; therefore I must tell you,

"That in the why,

So that no more of my kind will die,

I will not lie,

Crows may have, in their hatred and mischief, stolen eggs of the aliens without a good reason why."

Timothina then said,

"Gerald, we must talk to the one who knows.

And that is the way the wind of change blows.

Regardless of what is thought by the crows."

What is the secret message written in the earth?

With that, Gerald turned very quickly and left both Timothina and Timothy standing, speechless. Neither animal wanted to break the spell of what had just happened. They both stood still as if they were thinking; then in an instant Gerald flew and Timothy bounded after Timothina.

The cotton field had remained a cotton mulch field for a very long time.  It was as if the giants were waiting for something to happen before they planted the seeds. The days had started to grow longer and the nights and days, warmer.  Timothy looked for Gerald but could not find him.

The pheasants had started to nest in the hedgerow and were sitting on their eggs.  They were very careful to keep their eggs warm.  The male and female pheasants would take turns sitting on the eggs.  Timothy became very watchful because he did not want anything bad to happen to those pheasant eggs, and he also was anxious to talk to the wise old pheasant because he wanted to see if the wise old pheasant knew anything that could help the crows.

It was a rainy day in the hedgerow, and Timothy approached a pheasant hen sitting on her nest.  She started to cluck nervously as Timothy came closer.

Then she said, "That's close as you dare come, Timothy!  I know you are a special mouse of purpose, but I will attack you if you come one mouse step closer!"

Timothy stopped and asked her, "What is your name?"

"My name is Harmony, because I am the harmony pheasant. I provide a stable and understandable way that gives life to my chicks and harmony to the cotton field. After saying this she suddenly got off of her nest. Timothy backed up a bit. He was worried that she might attack. She did not attack; she just stood there by her nest while the rain fell on her eggs.

Find Harmony's name written in the clouds.

After a few nervous moments, Timothy got up the courage to ask her, "Why are you letting your eggs get wet?"

She answered, "My eggs need the moisture from the rain because the moisture keeps my eggshells from getting too hard and brittle. That way they will not break before it is time for my chicks to hatch."

"I am looking for the wise old pheasant; have you seen him?" Timothy asked.

"The wise old pheasant has left this farm because he needs more cover to hide in. I can remain because I am a hen, and the hunters do not hunt hens. Therefore, by remaining, I can make a harmonious environment."

Timothina, who was close by, said,

"Her feathers are of plain earth.

The giants know that she must give birth.

The harmony that she provides, gives our lives more worth.

The wise old pheasant is a cock who the giants want to kill,

Therefore the wise old pheasant must leave against his will.

And suffer the dearth

That has been brought about in the cotton field earth.

Timothy, as always, listened carefully to the poetical phrases of his sister. Then he said, "The harmony to which your name applies is threatened by something terrible that is happening to the crows. I must talk to the wise old pheasant because there is something that he knows that may be able to restore more harmony to our farm."

Harmony, did not like crows and she was especially afraid of them because they had stolen her eggs in the past, but she knew that if something terrible was happening to them that something would be terrible for all of the animals living on the farm. And after all, she was not called Harmony, for nothing.

Harmony, stood up very tall. She stretched out her neck. She pointed her beak to the sky, and she let out with two very loud pheasant chirps.

In the distance, Timothy heard two faint chirps in reply. Then he heard the distinctive explosive sound of a pheasant in flight, and in just moments standing before him and Timothina was the wise old pheasant.

Timothy was nervous about asking the wise old pheasant about the crows but he knew he had to help his friend Gerald, so he timidly asked, "Why are the crows getting sick and dying?"

The wise old pheasant had never looked more important or wise to Timothy. "Tlot, tlot, tlot, the crows are getting sick and dying because this family farm is very barren of food for them. Therefore they have started to eat the animal food by the little packages that the giants have put out in the industrial farm on the other side of the grey world. The giants of the industrial farm do not want to share with animals.

Timothy responded, "From what my mother told me, I understand, thank you, wise old pheasant."

With that, he and Timothina ran for the open field. Harmony and the wise old pheasant watched them go.

Harmony turned to the wise old pheasant, "Why would you ever help the crows?"

The wise old pheasant responded, "Timothy wants to end the war between us and the crows, and I also would like to see it end."

# Harrier Hawk

The two mice dashed into the mulched field with such speed that even the predators were taken by surprise. Most were not watching the open field in broad daylight because mice just normally would not so obviously expose themselves to danger.

These mice knew that they should not waste one second in telling the crows, because lives were on the line. When Timothina and Timothy reached the center of the cotton field, they were surprised to find Gerald already there waiting for them. Gerald tilted his head to the right, then to the left, and then touched his beak to the ground in front of Timothy and Timothina. Timothy and Timothina waited patiently, and then Timothy spoke, "The crows in your clan are getting sick and dying because of the food they are eating in the industrial farm on the other side of the grey world. It is food set by colorful little packages amongst the young corn plants."

"How did you find this out, Timothy?"

"I asked the wise old pheasant," Timothy responded.

"Thank you, Timothy and Timothina, you have done well," Gerald said in reply.

The Harrier hawk flew very low, looking for prey and hoping to find a fledgling crow or a field mouse.

When he passed over the hedgerow,

Can you see how perfectly aerodynamic this bird is for very fast flight?

he immediately saw the two field mice and the crow in the field. He sank lower in flight and picked up speed by the flapping of his wings. He needed to get a mouse before the crow could react. He had taken many fledgling crows for meals, but the adults were always a problem. Sometimes they would even go after him in flocks.

The attack came as a total surprise but Timothy and Timothina were saved by Gerald spotting the rapidly approaching shadow of the Harrier hawk.  Gerald knew from experience what the Harrier hawk shadow represented. He cawed a two-caw warning to the mice, and then he flew up and turned in mid air

to meet the glide path of the hawk.

Because the hawk could not rapidly change his course like the more agile crow he decided to take the crow that was directly in his glide path instead of the mouse.  He was concerned though because an adult crow could be very difficult to outmaneuver in the air. He was depending on the crow to become afraid, and thus, his glide path could remain unaltered until he struck.

Gerald, for his part, knew that he would lose if the hawk could get him with his talons or beak. He flew straight for the hawk, and just as they were to collide,

Can you already tell the difference in the maneuverability of these two birds?

Gerald did something that very few birds can do. He tumbled backward. As his talons came up, he clawed at the Harrier hawk.

124

The hawk was forced to strike back but his speed was no match for the talons of the tumbling crow. The two birds tumbled in aerial combat. They both stalled and were falling. The hawk screeched as he was forced to make a very rough landing.

Gerald righted himself in flight and flew away, making a rapidly repeated burst of two caws. Timothy and Timothina were safely back in their blackberry bush burrow before the aerial fight ended.

# Cotton Planting

When Timothy saw the tractor, he knew that the planting was to begin. The tractor moved slowly across the field. The cotton seeds were being planted in rows of eight. The seed hoppers were releasing just the right amount of seeds to plant two seeds each time the plunger went into the ground.

The earth which was moist from a recent rain smelled fresh and sweet to Timothy. He knew that the giants had chosen well for the day of planting. This day was always a special time for Timothy. It was the beginning of new life and adventure. Timothina watched the planting tractor with a sense of wonder.

"It is well to see,

That which will be.

What does this mean for us, Timothy?"

Timothy answered,

"Soon the new cotton will grow,

And only then will we know."

By the time the cotton was planted, the temperature had turned very mild.  It was warmer at night than it had been in a while, so Timothy and Timothina began to forage at night.

The night farm was very different from the farm in daylight.  Most of the birds slept from about sundown to sunup.  The birds that flew at night were the owls.  Of course the owls were extremely dangerous for mice, and Timothy and Timothina were very careful to stay hidden and extremely quiet.

# Moonlight and Friendship

The first cotton plants made their appearance after just a few days.  Timothy and Timothina still found it very difficult to forage in the open field with the threat of owls and other predators, so they remained in the hedgerow. Winter grasses and insects were their main source of food.

One night when the moon was full, Timothy was foraging when he chanced upon the wise old pheasant. He was surprised when he heard the familiar tlot, tlot, tlot, of his old friend.

What has happened to the complimentary colors of orange and blue in the moonlight?

"I thought that you would be sleeping wise old pheasant," Timothy said.

"I can't sleep," the wise old pheasant responded.

"Why, are you worried about the crows stealing your eggs?"

"No, the crows have stopped trying to steal our eggs," The wise old pheasant replied.

"That's probably because you helped them," Timothy said.

"Yes, I suppose so. I am afraid of the giants, Timothy. The cotton has started to grow, and soon they will come to hunt my kind," the wise old pheasant said.

"They have never been able to kill you; why do you think they can do it this time." Timothy remarked.

"Because of their dog Sunny; he is very good at finding me. In the past I have always been able to surprise them by running, but this time I believe they will be ready and will shoot me as I run."

"Don't worry, old friend, I have a plan," Timothy responded.  And with that he heard the wise old pheasant cluck softly and saw him turn his head and tuck his beak back in his feathers.  Soon the pheasant was asleep.

Timothina had listened in with a great deal of curiosity.

"What is you plan, brother dear?

Were you able to dispel his fear?"

"I believe I can create a surprise of my own." Timothy responded.

While the moon was yet full, Timothy led Timothina to the farmhouse, and there in the moonlight, the farmhouse looked totally different.

As is often the case with domestic cats, Patches was locked up for the night so that he wouldn't kill roosting birds.  Sunny was also inside the house where he was safe and warm.  Timothy and Timothina ran through the gate and into the sweet pea patch.  From the sweet pea patch, Timothy could see what he had come for.  There by Lucina's bicycle was one of Sunny's tennis balls.

Can you see the moonlit shadow of the walnut tree?

Timothy ran to the ball with Timothina. "We need to get this ball out into the cotton field!" Timothy told Timothina.

"We can push the ball,

All of the way.

Something we could not do at all,

If it was during the day," Timothina said.

"That is right,

But I am afraid of the owls in flight.

Timothina, we need help in our fight,

Or we could easily die tonight."

Timothy knew that Gerald usually roosted somewhere near the farmhouse because Gerald liked to be near Lucina. If only he could find his roost and wake him, maybe Gerald would be willing to help.

Timothy asked Timothina, "Where do you believe Gerald the crow might be roosting, because if we could wake him, maybe he would help us?

"If I were a crow,

High in the tree, I would go,

With feathers of black,

To conceal my back."

Timothina then noticed the dark forms in the moonlit shadow of the walnut tree, and when she looked up high in the walnut tree, they could see a thicketed area of dark forms. She said to Timothy,

"Brother, look up to the sky,

Because when I look up high,

I see forms in the tree

That look like crows to me."

Timothy looked up and could see the crows nested in the walnut tree. Timothy thought that among the crows in the nest, he might find Gerald. He stealthily moved close to the bottom of the walnut tree. Once there, he squeaked "Gerald!" One of the crows let loose

Can you find other night flying animals?

from an uppermost branch and silently glided to the ground.

"Timothy, what are you doing?"

Timothy was surprised because he had never seen a crow fly at night.

"Gerald, I was hoping you could help us, but I wasn't sure a crow could fly at night," Timothy said.

"Timothy, crows normally do not fly at night but sometimes, in the full moon we take flight and when we do, we are nearly invisible."

"Gerald I must get that ball that the dog chases out into the cotton field and I need your help. The owls or some other predator will get one or both of us if we try this without your help."

"Timothy I will be honored to fly in protection for you and your sister." And with that, Gerald flew into a low-lying branch of the bare walnut tree and stood guard for the two mice.

They ran to the nearby waiting ball. Timothy pushed the ball and started it rolling. He pushed it away from Lucina's bicycle and toward the gate.

What is causing Gerald's image to appear on the fence?

With a last big shove, he rolled the ball through the gate.

# Screech Owl

138

The moonlight shone brightly as Gerald watched the two mice taking turns pushing the ball making it more difficult to protect them. Moreover night predators could be nearly invisible and extremely fast. But Gerald knew what he needed to watch for.

Crows can be very good at keeping track of animals, and Gerald was an expert at following the habits, motion, and even personalities of animals. As the two mice moved further out into the field of baby cotton plants, they were ever more exposed to a fast-moving, or concealed predator. Gerald knew that if an attack came, he would need to be very close to the mice in order to help them. So as they moved, likewise he stayed in close proximity.

So there in the moonlight, two field mice and one crow worked their way out into the cotton field, moving along a golden retriever's favorite ball. The screech owl was hungry and she had chicks to feed. She had flown from her nest in a cavity in the side of a cottonwood tree by the river. She perched in the walnut tree after the three animals had already gone far out into the cotton field. The crows in the walnut tree woke and watched her very closely because in

spite of her small size, she could

Can you find the hidden message?

kill animals much larger than herself.

Like all owls, her night vision was excellent, and she could hear the mice and the crow as well. Even with great night vision, it was difficult to see the two black animals. Also, the sound the trio was making was somewhat confusing. The straining mice, the rolling ball, and the hopping crow were not making the usual steady sound pattern of a mouse.

She was hungry, though, and she could plainly see Timothy who, because of his lighter color and white marks, was easy to see in the moonlight. She took off and flew in a straight line for Timothy. The screech owl is very small but also an extremely fast flyer.

Gerald heard its wings as the owl took off. He only had time to save one mouse, and if he made the wrong choice, the other mouse would die because the owl had already chosen its target and could not change course. Because Timothy was lighter in color, he guessed that the owl had chosen Timothy, so he picked Timothy up, lifted him a few feet and gently dropped him. The screech owl came down with talons outstretched where Timothy had been.

Confused, the screech owl hopped around, but on the ground, she was no match in speed to the fleeing mice. So after a few hops, she flew away in search of another larger prey animal. Gerald simply changed course and flew back to his roost where he quickly went back to sleep in the walnut tree in the company of his crow clan.

The ball was now well out in the cotton field,  so Timothy and Timothina did not return to the ball for some time.

# Cotton Squares

As the weather warmed, the young cotton plants grew quickly and leafed out.  Soon there was enough cover in the cotton field for the mice to return to foraging there.  The cotton plants had very large leaves.  The stems very rapidly grew extremely strong and fibrous.  The plants also became quite tall, and for mice, they appeared like small trees.

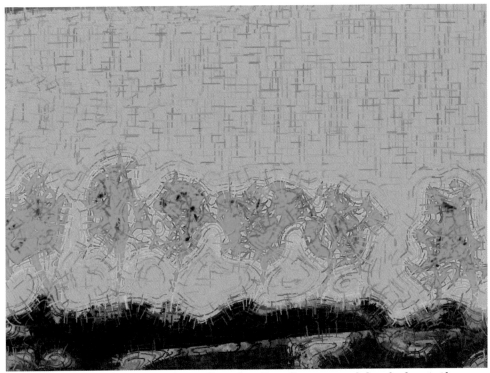

The mice kept hoping for fruit of some kind, but the only thing that appeared were very small, hard, leafy

squares.  The two mice studied the leafy squares, but they knew by their odor that they would not be good to eat, and they also realized that they were the beginnings of what would be cotton flowers.

The plants were stronger than tomato and wheat plants and not nearly as tall as corn plants. They were fun to climb and play on. Also there were a great many insects that frequented the plants, and some of the insects were good to eat. But many of the insects were not good to eat, and some of those, like the wasps and lady bugs, were protecting the cotton plants by eating harmful insects. Being a successful wild field mouse required understanding the insect world in great detail. Timothy had learned to tell the difference, for the farm plants, between harmful insects and beneficial insects. So he passed this knowledge on to Timothina as he also showed her how to forage for plant food that the giants of the farm were not cultivating.

Like the tomato field, Timothy found the cotton plants very pleasant. They made a soft rustling noise in the breeze, they smelled really fresh, and they were very beautiful to look at. Timothina like Timothy, paid a great deal of attention to her favorite cotton plants. It came as a terrible shock to her when one day, she saw one of her favorite plants with utterly destroyed squares.  The plant had changed from a beautiful tall plant with wonderful even squares to a withered limp plant with brown and rotting squares.

She was frantic with sadness.  She cut off a stem

with the rotten squares with her teeth and carried it to her brother.

"Here you can see

Something that is terrible to me.

I found my favorite cotton plant-tree.

With squares attacked most deadly.

Brother dear,

My favorite cotton plant-tree is gone,

What could this destruction be based upon?"

Timothy answered, "Timothina dear, we must understand what you have found here.  We must find the wise old pheasant and ask him about this.

The two mice then each carried a destroyed cotton stem in search of the wise old pheasant.

Near the farmhouse in the hedgerow, they found the wise old pheasant.  He was staring at the farmhouse and seemed lost in thought.

"Tlot, tlot, tlot, why are you carrying cotton plant stems?"  the wise old pheasant asked Timothy and Timothina.

Timothina answered,

"Wise old pheasant, the one who knows,

Something is amiss here as it grows.

This plant was so beautiful to the eye.

What is causing it to die?"

The pheasant studied the cotton squares. Then he pecked the rotten squares. As he pecked the squares and they fell apart. The mice knew instantly why the cotton plant had become so sick and died.

Inside the squares were hideous-looking boll weevil larvae.

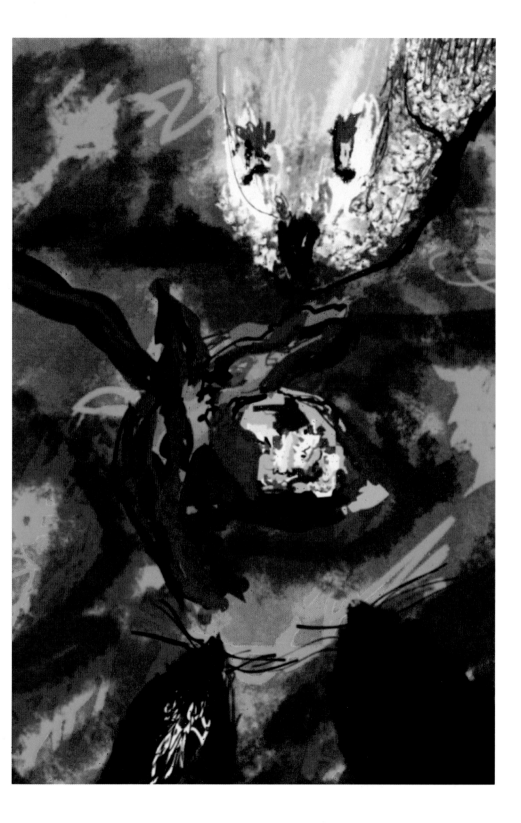

The wise old pheasant spoke, "Timothina dear, this is bad news, indeed, for you have found the boll weevil here. All of the cotton plants could die as this one did. You must somehow help the giants to know that the hideous weevil is in the cotton field"

Timothy asked, "Did these grow from the eggs of the horrible-looking insect with the long beak?"

"Yes, Timothy, that's the boll weevil," answered the wise old pheasant. Then he went on to say something that may have revealed why he was looking at the farmhouse with such a faraway look in his eyes. "If the cotton plants all die, this farm could be lost, and if that happens, the giant's family farm could be taken over by the industrial farmers."

With that, Timothina said,

"We thank you wise old pheasant.

Even though this news is highly unpleasant.

We will go to warn the giants, as you say,

So that our family farm will not be taken away."

The mice picked up the infected cotton plant stems and went toward the farmhouse. The cover was much better now that the cotton plants were taller, so the mice were able to get quite close to the house without worrying so much about predators.

They knew that they had to put the infected plants by the farmhouse for Lucina to see. But how could they accomplish this without the cat or dog attacking them?

They decided to ask Gerald for help. The crows had returned to the cotton field because now, with the young cotton plants taller and other plants growing in the field, there were plenty of insects and young plants of other varieties to forage on. Also, the mice suspected that the crows had learned from Gerald to avoid the industrial farm.

When sunset came, they saw Gerald land in his favorite roosting place. They could tell it was Gerald because his landing seemed more assured and direct than the other crows.

When he landed, Timothy let out his loudest squeak. Gerald immediately recognized Timothy's call, flew directly down and landed in front of the two mice. Gerald tilted his head to the right, to the left, then he touched his beak to the ground in front of the two waiting mice.

"Why have you called me?" Gerald asked.

Timothina ran up in front of Gerald and dropped the infected stem. Gerald looked down and said, "The work of the boll weevil, no doubt."

"Yes, and now you can see,

Why we have asked you down from your tree."

Please, friend crow,

Fly these squares to an obvious place

So that Lucina can know,

With what danger they are laced." Timothina said.

When Timothina finished speaking, Gerald picked up one of the infected stems with the pathetic-looking squares and flew off to the porch of the farmhouse.

He returned and flew the second stem to the same place so that when Lucina left the house, she could not help but to see them. Then he flew to his perch and was asleep by the time the sun finally set.

The mice knew that Lucina was usually the first of the giants to come out of the farmhouse in the morning. She was up early and always wanted to visit Starlight the horse and play with Sunny the dog before her day began.

This matter of the boll weevil was so important that the mice decided to wait nearby until the next morning to make sure that Lucina found the infected squares.  It was after early morning foraging in the cotton field, at about the time the sun was to come up, that the mice found themselves at the edge of the cotton field watching the front door of the farmhouse.

Suddenly Lucina came running out of the house with Sunny the dog.  She had two balls in her hands and she was intent on throwing them for Sunny to retrieve.  She ran right over the tops of the two stems with their infected squares without even noticing them.

"What can we do, Timothy?

These squares, she must see," Timothina said.

"We must do something to draw her attention to the squares, or all will be lost," Timothy responded.

It was then that Timothy decided to do something that a prudent field mouse should never do.  He ran straight for the porch. In broad daylight, with little cover, he had decided that drawing Lucina's attention to the infected squares was more important than his own life.

Timothina was much faster than Timothy, and she caught up with him in an instant.

"Timothy dear,

Please do not be rash in your fear.

For Gerald the crow is already here," Timothina whispered in his ear as she ran close to him.

Timothy stopped, and sure enough he could see Gerald on the porch next to the infected stems. Gerald let out two loud caws, over and over again.

Lucina heard Gerald. She threw the ball for Sunny in order to divert his attention, and then she ran to the porch to see what Gerald was so upset about. Gerald stayed right there by the squares. Upon her arrival, Gerald tilted his head to the right, then to the left, and then he touched his beak to the squares in front of Lucina and he pecked them.

She looked down and saw the problem.   Gerald cawed twice and flew to his roost in the walnut tree.

Lucina picked up the stems and studied the squares. She carefully pulled apart the lips of the squares and saw the multitude of boll weevil larvae.  She ran back in to the house yelling, "Daddy, Daddy!"

"What, Lucina?" her father answered.

"Look, Daddy Gerald the crow brought me these squares.  This is horrible; something has gotten into our cotton plants and could destroy our whole crop. What could cause this kind of an infection?"

Lucina's father took one of the infected squares and studied it carefully. Then he said, "Lucina this is the work of the boll weevil. We have a serious problem on our hands. In Alabama and other southern states, during the early 20$^{th}$ century, the boll weevil invaded from Mexico and decimated the cotton fields. Fortunately, today, we have organic methods of dealing with the threat of the boll weevil."

"We will plant a trap crop of corn in order to entice the weevil to infect the corn instead of the cotton plants, and we will also spray the cotton plants with an organic insecticide so that we rid ourselves of the harmful insects without leaving toxic residue in the cotton plants."

"Are you sure this will work, Daddy?" Lucina asked.

"Yes, I am sure Lucina. You know in Enterprise Alabama in, 1919, the citizens erected a monument to the boll weevil.

What kind of a hat is the lady of the boll weevil monument holding and why?

It is the only monument erected to honor an insect that I know of anywhere."

"Why did they make a monument to honor the boll weevil Dad?"

"Because in the southern states, where cotton was such an important crop, the boll weevil caused such devastation to the cotton crops that it forced the farmers to diversify the kinds of crops that they planted. When the farmers only planted cotton, the boll weevil found a perfect environment to thrive."

"As a result of the devastation caused by the boll weevil plague, the farmers started growing peanuts, sorghum, okra and other crops. By diversifying and rotating the types of crops that they planted, they were able to control the boll weevil population and their agricultural way of life became even stronger and more prosperous."

"Our best defense against pests like the boll weevil is to rotate our crops because the varied habitats created by the rotation of crops do not provide an ideal environment for any single pest. When crops are rotated and all of the creatures on the farm are preserved, a healthy balance is maintained between predators and prey, and it is balance in nature that ensures the long-term health of the farm."

Lucina had confidence in her dad, but she was still very worried about the cotton field and what the boll weevil could do to the plants and the future of their family farm.  She was also very grateful to the crow that she had named Gerald for bringing her the infected squares.

# Cotton Flowers

Timothy and Timothina returned to their burrow and fell asleep, confident that the giants were aware of the threat of the long-beaked insect.  Timothina dreamt of buzzing insects and flowers.

The tractor moved quickly along the edge of the cotton field, plowing a fresh growing area.  Timothy could not understand why the giants were turning over everything along the edge of the cotton field long before the young cotton plants could produce anything but squares.  However, his instincts told him that the giants were doing something to protect the young cotton plants from the boll weevil.

The giants plowed, built furrows, planted corn and irrigated the edge of the field.  They also walked through the field spraying the young cotton plants with organic pesticide. Timothy and Timothina could tell that the spray was intended to repel and kill the boll weevil and other harmful insects.

When the mice found the wise old pheasant, they asked him about the changes in the cotton field. He told them, "The giants are spraying with a special type of plant juice than can repel and kill the boll weevil, as well as other insects that can harm the cotton plants. Along the edge of the cotton field, they are planting a trap crop of corn. They are not spraying the corn so that harmful insects will prefer it to the cotton."

It seemed to happen all at once. The cotton plants burst forth with flowers. The field smelled wonderfully fragrant. There was a wonderful exuberance in the air.

A giant came to the field in a truck loaded with white boxes. The giant unloaded the boxes and placed them in the hedgerow next to the cotton field. The giant who worked with the white boxes was covered with a white skin and had a large covering over his head.

Can you find bees in this illustration?

The mice were curious about the white boxes. When the giant left the white boxes behind, the mice ran to a place as close to the boxes as they could get. The buzzing noise was deafening. Bees were going and coming from the white boxes. They were flying to the cotton plants, burring themselves in the flowers and then returning to their hives in the boxes. The mice could smell that there was something very sweet and good to eat inside the boxes.

With whiskers twitching, the two mice approached the white boxes.

"Timothy, the delicious sweet smell,

I can imagine the taste of this food so well," Timothina said.

The odor was like a magnet that drew the two mice forward. "Timothina, maybe there is a way to get some of this wonderful food that the bees are making," Timothy said.

The two curious mice had no idea of what they were up against in trying to steal honey from the hive. Timothy edged closer and closer, hoping to find an opening into the box through which he could get to the delicious smelling food inside.

Something about the brown color of the small mammal approaching the hive deeply bothered the guardian bee, and he decided that the brown mouse had crossed the line. He was a threat to the hive.

He flew straight as an arrow and landed on Timothy's back and stung him.

Timothy squeaked in pain, and ran. Timothina could have easily outrun him but she was worried about her brother. She ran ahead of him but close enough for him to follow. She could sense that he was in terrible pain. By this time, there was a whole swarm of bees pursuing the fleeing mice. The mice were faster than the bees, and fortunately, Timothina, who always thought so quickly, lead her brother down a gopher hole. The bees continued to buzz around the opening but did not go into the hole.

Safely down in the gopher hole, Timothy told his sister, "I feel very sick, and I do not know if I am going to ever get better."

"Brother, you cannot leave me,

Without you, I would be so lonely.

But where I should go,

I do not know."

Timothy was feeling very sick and drowsy. He could barely stand the pain. He was getting weaker by the minute. He tried to talk to Timothina, but the words would not come out. He slipped from consciousness. He saw his green jade cross above a portal. He wanted to run through the portal to the beautiful wild world that he could see on the other side, but all of a sudden, in front of the portal, was the shaman with the crow feathers in his hair.

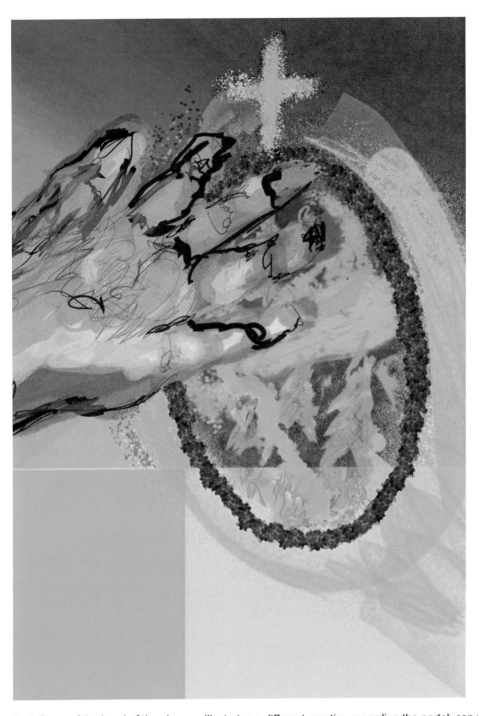

Each finger of the hand of the shaman illustrates a different emotion regarding the portal; can you describe those emotions finger by finger?

He put his hand over the portal and spoke to Timothy so that he could understand perfectly, "Timothy, I know that you want to flee through that portal, but you must not. You and your sister still have much of your purpose to fulfill. She cannot make it without you. Wake up! Tell Timothina to pull the stinger from your back and make a poultice of willow leaves."

The willow is the shrub-like tree that grows by the edge of where the water flows through the irrigation ditch. It is the tree with the long pointed leaves. She must chew the willow leaf and put it where the stinger was pulled. She has very little time to help you stay on this side of the portal to pure wilderness from which you will not be able to return."

Timothy forced himself back to consciousness. In a very weak voice, he said, "Sister, please pull the stinger from my back."

Timothina quickly found the end of the stinger and used her little mouse hand to pull it from Timothy's back. Timothy had fallen asleep again.

Timothina knew instinctively that if she let him sleep, he would probably not wake up.

She took his little mouse head in her hands and shook it. "Wake up! Wake up! You must wake up Timothy," she yelled as she shook his head.

Timothy awoke from his stupor, but he was very sick. "Please, Timothina, go to the tree with the long pointed leaves that grows by the irrigation ditch. Cut a leaf with your teeth and chew it; then put it on my back where the stinger was pulled."

Timothina ran like the wind to the edge of the irrigation ditch and there she found the bush-like tree with the pointed leaves.

Can you find the name of this particular tree?

She climbed the trunk of the willow and then climbed to a leaf stem. She chewed the stem until the leaf fell to the muddy ground below. She became frantic, for she knew that time was running out for Timothy. She dropped to the ground, picked up the leaf and ran with it in her mouth back to where Timothy lay. She chewed the leaf to a wet pulp, mixing it with her saliva.

She used her little mouse hands to pack the chewed-up willow leaf on his wound. Timothy's body had become very cold. She put her body over the poultice and next to his to warm him and then she waited. In the hours that passed, the chemicals in the willow leaf worked to counteract the poison by reducing the swelling and relieving the pain. After several hours, she felt his body start to warm.

Eventually Timothy awoke. He weakly said, "Thank you, Timothina you saved my life." And he fell back to sleep. For two days, Timothy was so weak that he could not forage for himself. Timothina continued to pack the stinger wound with willow poultice and brought plant food and insects to the gopher hole for him to eat. Gradually, Timothy regained his strength.

When Timothy finally looked out of the makeshift burrow, he could not believe his eyes.  What a sight!

When Timothy looks out, what animal can he see that helps to pollinate the cotton flowers?

The cotton field was ablaze with cotton flowers. And, for a mouse with such a great sense of smell, the scent of the cotton flowers was intoxicating. Timothy was back!  He felt like a new mouse and he was so grateful to his sister for saving his life.

As he did when he was a younger cornfield mouse, he started to climb the cotton stalks. He was amazed by how beautiful the cotton plants were with their beautiful white flowers with grey-green stalks and large leaves.

Being part of the flowering cotton field made the mice feel exuberant and strong.  They would swing on the plants and grab a leaf with their hands and bounce up and down before they let go to sail to the ground.  Timothina said,

"Timothy, this is so much fun,

We can play bounce and then run.

I wish we could do this until the there is no more sun.

And then we can play so more in the light of the moon.

I know that our play will end too soon!"

The mice explored the cotton flowers and found them fragrant and fun to play with.

They were especially smooth and translucent, so they felt good to both rub against and try to look through.

These were great times in the cotton field. The plants were young, fragrant, and beautiful. The mice were healthy, and they felt very secure because the robust young plants made it nearly impossible for the predators to find them. Flower health and beauty goes hand in hand with animal health, beauty and mouse security.

I guess you could say that Timothina said it best when she told Timothy,

"I love the smell and sight of the cotton,

It seems that this kind of a world can never be forgotten,

The flowers are so beautiful and new,

I am so happy that to their welfare we have been true.

When the cotton waves in the breeze,

We feel like we are in a forest of magnificent cotton trees.

I am so happy to be with my brother dear,

And I hope that somehow we can always hold the cotton field near."

But as the cotton flowers wave in the breeze this cotton flower spell will be lost I fear."

This last stanza of her poem foretold the change was on its way, because cotton flowers must give way to cotton bolls. And with the cotton bolls, a whole new world would envelope the cotton field.

# Cotton Bolls

When the cotton flowers dried out, the large hips at the bottom of the cotton flower seemed to get bigger and bigger.

Timothy wondered, "Are these bolls going to turn red like the green tomatoes did?"

One day when the mice were foraging in the cotton field, they came upon Sunny's tennis ball. Timothy told Timothina, "Now that we have better cover, we must move this ball closer to the hedgerow." Timothina asked,

"Why is this ball so important,

What can be its intent?"

Timothy answered,

"I believe this ball has a role to play, that will keep all our foes at bay." With that, the two mice took turns they rolling the ball until it was very close to the hedgerow.

Soon after this, Lucina came through the cotton field with her father.  They were carefully inspecting the bolls that had formed when the flowers dried out, looking for insect damage.   Lucina's father said, "Lucina, these bolls look good!"   Lucina replied, "Yes Daddy, I am so relieved."

As they worked their way through the field, Lucina was getting very close to the mice.  Finally, she was so close that they had to choose whether to run or possibly let her see them.  Timothina asked her brother,

"Timothy,

Should we run with the giants so near,

Or stay here and face our fear?"

Timothy replied, "Let's stay, because this is who carried us to safety in her hands.

So the two mice remained on the cotton plants that they were climbing, and sure enough, Lucina saw them. "Daddy, Daddy, look, here are Timothy and Timothina. I can tell it is them because Timothy has those white scratch marks on him, and Timothina is black as can be."

Her father replied, "That's interesting, Lucina, they are probably harmless to the cotton plants, and who knows, maybe they are doing some good. After all, I am sure they must eat some harmful insects."

Lucina wanted to hold the mice, but she resisted the temptation because she knew how important it was that they remain wild and free. She said as she left, "I believe somehow you mice are fulfilling an important purpose." Timothy wished he could understand what she was trying to say but he could not. Timothina was kind of sad to see her go walking away, continuing to carefully separate the cotton plants and inspect the bolls. And she wondered,

"With this girl walking away,

Find the word that describes the mood of coming change?

Is there something more to this day?

Are we also are moving away?

Is there a climax to the cycle of cotton growth,

That will somehow change us both?"

# Cotton

As was the case with the corn, tomato, and wheat fields, the cotton field was slowly drying out. The days were getting longer and warmer. Foraging was becoming more difficult for all of the birds and mammals. There were fewer insects and the cotton plants seemed to be totally inedible. The plants swayed as the dry wind wafted through the field.

Timothy and Timothina were foraging in the cotton field when Timothy saw his first open cotton boll.

It was an amazing sight to behold. Inside the open boll were the prettiest white fibers. He climbed the cotton plant and went out on the stem.

Timothina said, "Timothy what is happening to the bolls?

Where the flowers were, are now holes,

And the white fibers I see,

For what use could they be?

They sure look pretty!

But, are they ready?"

Timothy continued to investigate the cracked boll with the exposed fibers. "What were they?" he thought. Then he sniffed them; incredibly, they had almost no odor. He nibbled at them to see if they were good to eat, but they had no flavor. He remembered what the wise old pheasant had told him a long time ago, "The giants grow cotton for their extra skins."

He decided that things would not get better for foraging because it seemed that these plants were not something animals could use for food. He knew from experience that when the crops started to dry and a harvest was near, usually things were quite good for animals, but this was different. He then remembered something else that the wise old pheasant had told him, "Cotton is a very different kind of crop that always brings with it a great deal of turmoil."

# Ground Squirrels

One day, when Lucina was inspecting the cotton field, she heard a loud chirping. She knew that even though it sounded like a bird, it was not! It was the California ground squirrel. She knew that they could eat the cotton plants and destroy the roots. They were so aggressive they could even invade the farmyard and house. Also, their tunneling could undermine the foundation of the farmhouse. Sunny and Patches had done a good job keeping them out of the farmyard, but her fear was that the ground squirrels were invading the cotton field.

She worked her way carefully through the cotton plants to find the source of the chirping, all the while hoping that she was wrong about identifying it as the sound of a ground squirrel. She kept hoping that maybe it was the call of a bird or something else.

What she saw next made her feel sick. There, in the midst of the cotton field, was a large mound, and around the mound, with its ground squirrel holes, were many dead cotton plants and one ground squirrel, staring defiantly at her.

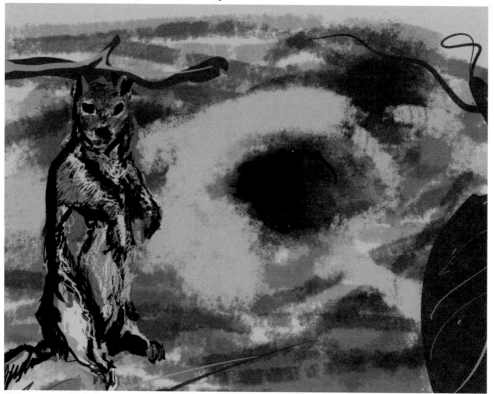

She quickly worked her way to the edge of the field and ran back to the house to tell her father.

"Lucina, why are you running so hard?" her dad said.

"I have found a ground squirrel and his mound in the cotton field. With these dry hot conditions, I am afraid we have just the right conditions for the ground squirrels to invade the cotton field."

Her father replied, "I will set some live traps so that we can move some of them to an appropriate place in the foothills where the predator/prey relationship can keep their population in balance, but in the end, we also are going to need some help from coyotes that roam this field." Lucina and her father went to collect their live traps to put out in the cotton field.

# Rex

Rex the coyote was in some ways like Gerald the crow. He was unusual for his species. He was extremely intelligent, which is common for coyotes but like Gerald the crow, he could think beyond just what was necessary to stay alive. Like all coyotes, he was mostly carnivorous, but for some reason, he did not like to kill and eat mice, which made him highly unusual for a coyote because sometimes coyotes feed almost entirely on mice. Instead he hunted larger animals, deer, rabbits and squirrels, and that is probably how he was able to relate to Timothy without killing him.

Rex normally stayed away from farm fields because the larger prey animals that he hunted were usually found in open fields and the riparian areas by the river. It was only by a strange coincidence that he met Timothy.

He had been hunting rabbits along the riverbank and had decided to follow an irrigation ditch in the hopes of finding a rabbit or squirrel. The irrigation ditch that he was following this night was the one that ran through the middle of the hedgerow where Timothy and Timothina had their burrow. It was one of those special nights when the moon was full, the air was clear, and the cotton plants were still, with their shadows, creating a marvelous texture of lines, light and dark. It was one of those special moments that could bring a coyote to sing, and sing to the moon Rex did.

He yipped, he yelped, he barked, and he howled. It was a beautiful coyote worship song inspired by the balance of nature and the moon. Both Timothy and

Timothina were taken by it. They were mesmerized by the sound and the magic of the moonlit night.

They drew closer to the coyote, and finally, Timothy could stand it no longer. He stood up on his hind legs and with his little mouse voice, howled to the moon. Timothina joined in, and there they stood right out in the open, where Rex could see them acting as if they were both coyotes. They howled and sang to the moon with the coyote.

Can you find a mouse howling at the moon with Rex?

Rex looked over at them. "You must be Timothy the magical mouse," he said. "I did not believe Strand's stories but I have remained curious about a magical mouse ever since I heard Strand carry on."

"You must be the magical mouse because only a magical mouse would be so brave or crazy to stand out in the open and sing to the moon with a coyote!"

"I am not magical; however, I have been very fortunate when a particular fox has tried to take me. I have never known his name. Some animals that I have met do say that I have a purpose which I also do not understand. My name is Timothy and this is my sister Timothina," Timothy replied.

"Well, coyotes have a rule, Timothy. If any animal participates in the celebration of a special moment with the moon, we must respect that animal as one of our own. So I welcome you and your sister to the clan of the coyote. If you two were not animals of purpose, you would have never joined me in the song of celebration that we sing to the moon. You are the first animals other than coyotes that I have ever seen do such a thing, and I will have to think more about what this portends. My name is Rex, and I am at your service." And after saying that, Rex tilted his head as he looked at them with a strange kind of knowing look in his eye

 and then disappeared, trotting of into the moonlight down the hedgerow toward the river.

"What has happened here is magical, Timothy,

If what has happened can actually be.

What a mystery!

If our purpose the animals understand,

What is that ties us together as a band,

To this family's farmland?"

Timothy simply answered, "I do not know, sister."
The mice left the magical place and moment in the
hedgerow and went out into the cotton field to
forage. They were deep into the cotton field when
they could smell the distinctive odor of another type
of rodent.

Timothina said to Timothy, "What kind of an animal
can this be?

For I have never smelled this type of scent,
Timothy."

"I do not know, but this is not good I fear," Timothy
responded.

Following this new scent, they went further into the
cotton field. The moonlight revealed the scene of
destruction. The mounds, the holes in the ground,
and the scattered dead cotton plants were plainly

visible.

The mice did not utter a word out of fear of being detected by whatever had caused such destruction! They both knew that the animals were a type of rodent like themselves, but what type? Timothy thought of Willow the field rat, but Willow could never do anything like this.

These field mice had done everything they could to preserve their wild farm home. Timothy had stood up to tomato worms, grasshoppers, a cat bird, and the boll weevil. He was not about to let these rodents, whoever they were, destroy the cotton field. But what could he do?

"They are sleeping," he whispered to Timothina.

She did not answer but rather switched to a silent mental telepathy with her brother that animals are so good at. She could sense he wanted her to stay while he explored the den of the mysterious sleeping animals.

He entered the tunnel with his whiskers twitching and nose working overtime. It was very dark, but Timothy had excellent night vision. Slowly he crept forward.

Rex had left the field mice and the moon celebration and was heading for the river. The night had been very still, but as often happens in the night, a slight breeze had picked up. Rex caught the faint scent of what he had been hoping to smell. It was very faint, but it came from the cotton field.

He changed course and started to follow the scent into the cotton field.

Timothy had not gone very far into the tunnel when he heard the rapid movement of a large rodent.  He spun around and ran for his life.  He made it out into the open, but there he was confronted by the ground squirrel.  He stopped short.

The ground squirrel pursuing him also stopped. Timothy was now between two ground squirrels. The one behind him said, "This is my kill, I found him first."

The ground squirrel in front of him said, "Forget it Jerry this mouse is mine!"

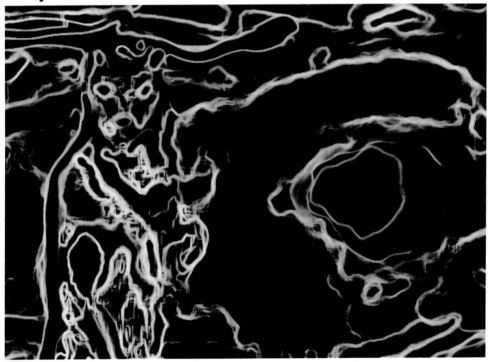

"Okay, just let me kill him first so he doesn't escape; then we can fight over him," Jerry said.

This statement gave Jerry pause, and both ground squirrels started to circle with Timothy stuck in the middle.

Ajax, the other ground squirrel, was known for his ability to fight, and Jerry did not want to wind up as a meal for Ajax, but on the other hand, he did not want to lose this delicious mouse meal. So they circled each other with Timothy stuck in the middle.

Timothina watched, hidden in the cotton plants at the edge of this cotton field arena of combat. She was desperate to save her brother, and in her poetical mind, ideas were flooding in from many different directions. Timothina was so fast partly because she could be so unconventional for a mouse. She really did not have to wait for a routine in order to act. She yipped at the moon, then she said,

"Why fight to the death for Timothy,

When one of you can have me."

With that, she stepped out into the arena. Ajax really did not want to bother with another mouse, and he was sure he could best Jerry in a fight. Jerry, on the other hand, was hungry, and it seemed to him like a better option to catch the black mouse than fight with Ajax over the brown mouse. So he said, "If you really want to offer yourself to me in order to try to save this mouse you call Timothy, please come a little closer because I do not want to have to chase you that far because I am quite hungry."

Timothina ran right toward him. Jerry paused, surprised by this seemingly insane behavior for a field mouse. His pause gave Timothy the break he was looking for; he also ran toward Jerry and that confused him even more.

Timothina turned quickly and ran into the cotton field. Now both mice were in the high cotton plants running for their lives. Jerry was chasing Timothina and Ajax was chasing Timothy.

Rex knew he was getting closer to the ground squirrel mounds because their odor was getting stronger. Then he heard Timothina's yip, yip, yip and also the sound of the circling and talking squirrels. His trot changed to a run as he gained on his target by sound and smell.

Timothina was so fast that Jerry could not keep up, Ajax, though, was gaining ground on Timothy and was about to make his kill when he felt the coyote's teeth close on his neck. Ajax did not suffer because the coyote kill was instant. It was the in the code of the coyote to never let a prey animal suffer.

Timothy stopped and turned. Rex dropped the limp Ajax to the ground. "Timothy said, "Thank you, Rex!" Rex tilted his head to the side as he had done when they parted last and he had that same knowing look in his eyes. Then he said something that Timothy would never forget, "I will see you later, brother mouse." With that he picked up the dead ground squirrel and disappeared into the high cotton plants.

# Defoliant

The field mice never saw another coyote, but they smelled the odor of coyotes in the cotton field more than before. They knew that they had come for the ground squirrels, field rats and field mice, so they foraged more carefully since not all of the coyotes would understand the pact that they had with Rex. Soon when the mice approached the decimated area of the cotton field where the ground squirrels had been, they could not scent any more squirrels.

The cotton field continued to get dryer. The days were getting longer and hotter. Foraging was becoming more difficult among the withered cotton plants.

It was one of those dry hot days when the mice saw their first dry cotton ball.

 It is hard to imagine how strange and beautiful the cotton looked. It wasn't a type of fruit, it wasn't a

vegetable, and it wasn't a flower. It was something else. It sort of reminded Timothy of something from the golden world at the top of the corn plants. It was the way the sunlight passed through the cotton, giving it a crystalline beauty.

One day when Timothy and Timothina were foraging in the hedgerow, they heard what sounded like a very powerful and fast tractor. The sound approached so quickly that the mice were forced to look up to follow it. They saw an amazing sight, "a flying tractor."

The flying tractor was spraying the cotton plants. The spray smelled very salty to the mice. They had never seen a flying tractor, and they immediately had many questions about it and the salty-smelling spray. This flying tractor meant change of a different sort, and they went looking for answers from the wise old pheasant.

They found him talking to one of Harmony's pheasant pullets. "Tlot, tlot, tlot, when the hunters come with their dogs, you will be terrified, but you must not fly.  Wait until they are very close and then before the dogs point you out, *run through thick grass and weeds*!  It will be very difficult, but if you do not listen to me, you will die," he told the young pullet.

Listening to this conversation made Timothy think of Sunny the dog.  When the mice were very close, the wise old pheasant said, "Tlot, tlot,tlot, it is good to see that you are both alive and healthy.  Do you have a question?"

Timothy responded, "We want to know about the flying tractor and why the giants are spraying the cotton plants."

"Tlot, tlot, tlot, the flying tractor is a bird machine with two wings that the giants can use in order to fly slowly and close to the ground for spraying.  The giants are using it to spray the leaves of the cotton plants so that they will fall off quicker than normal. They do that so that their ground machines can pick the cotton. The cotton is used to make their extra skins and also..." But the wise old pheasant did not finish the sentence because something frightened him and he exploded into flight.

Timothy wondered what the wise old pheasant was about to say, but he understood that the pheasant was getting very jumpy because soon the giants were going to try to kill him again. It wasn't long though until the mice understood the unfinished sentence.

They were foraging in the cotton field at night when it was cooler and they were less visible to predators. The moonlight had a way of turning the cotton balls into magic lanterns of diffused light. Timothy climbed the stalk of a particularly beautiful cotton plant that was now starting to shed its dried leaves. He climbed out on a stem to the cracked boll and the magic light that seemed to come from the cotton.

As he got closer he smelled something he had

never smelled before. It had a very appetizing oily scent to it. He followed his nose into the cotton, and there he encountered the source of the aroma. He used one of his mouse hands to reach into the cotton and grab it. He then nibbled it. What a discovery! It was a delicious cotton seed. At last he had found an edible part to the cotton plants.

After that Timothy and Timothina found it very easy to live off of the cotton seeds. By eating a seed or two, they were mightily energized.

# Dry Cotton

The mice were not the only animals to discover the hidden treasure inside the cotton. Many types of birds invaded the cotton field in search of the cotton seeds. Timothy knew that these birds were a problem for the giants just as the cat bird had been for the grape grower.

He could not help but like the little finches though. They were so pretty in their various colors and so full

of life. Also the finches were very helpful to the field mice because they were so sensitive that whenever something was even near the cotton field, they would fly up in mass and serve as a warning to the mice.

When the hunters entered the cotton field, the finches called their warning tweets and flew furiously away.

Can you find the hidden white rabbit?

Timothy and Timothina knew that the time of the hunters had come, and they ran to find the wise old pheasant. When they found him in a thick bunch of grass in the hedgerow, Timothina spoke,

"Dear wise old pheasant,

We know this day will not be pleasant.

But with us you must stay,

If you are to survive this day.

And survive you can,

Because we have a plan,

That can foil the dog,

If you are by the log.

You must follow us,

To a place that you can trust.

When the timing for escape is at its peak,

We will sound our combined squeak,

So that you will know when to run,

From the hunter's gun."

The wise old pheasant walked nervously behind his two friends to a place behind a log and near the waiting tennis ball. There he squeezed in tight to the ground, hidden by the log and the tall grass.

The mice went to the tennis ball and waited. Some hunters walked the cotton field and some, the hedgerow. As shots were fired, the mice knew animals were dying. They would hear the explosion of pheasant wings, then the shots.

Timothy then remembered how a long time ago, he had asked the councilor rat, "Are the giants predators?" and she had answered, "Yes and no." He understood that though he had never seen them chase an animal like the fox or coyote, they could indeed behave as predators, but their ways of killing were very strange. They used guns, machines and poisoned animal food so that they did not kill directly, using teeth or claws. Also he could not be sure they killed for food or protection as other predators did. Now he understood why the councilor rat had to pause and think before saying, "Yes and no," in answer to his question.

The hunters and their dogs were getting closer and closer. The two mice and the wise old pheasant were frozen in anticipation. Sunny broke through the cotton and started to follow the scent left by the wise old pheasant as he had hopped to the log. She was very close. One of the hunters said, "Jim, be ready because I have missed my bird twice because he has run on me rather than flown. If Sunny flushes him we can get him on the ground!"

Sunny was just about to point at the log when the two mice together pushed the tennis ball down a slight grade. It started to roll. Sunny caught the motion of the ball out of the side of her eye. She instantly turned and ran for the ball. One of the hunters said, "Look, Jim, she has caught the scent get ready!"

But Sunny did not point; she picked up the tennis ball and ran back to the hunters. "No! Sunny, no Sunny," one of the hunters yelled, but Sunny just ran up to the hunter and dropped the ball at his feet, while wagging his tail, hoping that the hunter would throw it for him to retrieve.

None of the hunters heard the high-pitched combined squeaks of the two field mice or noticed the deeper grass and plants part as the wise old pheasant made his getaway.  The wise old pheasant did not stop running and flying until he reached a refuge, a place where hunters never came. The wise old pheasant ran right under a sign that said, "Posted No Hunting! Wildlife Refuge."

The wise old pheasant had learned to stay there until the sounds and smell of the hunting season for pheasants had ceased.

# Cotton Harvest

This hunting season came to an end and a beautiful light fell over the cotton field.  The cotton reflected and diffused the sunlight.  The gentle wind blew the cotton around so that it appeared like a field of wondrous iridescent pearls.  The animals could sense that the harvest was coming, and with that, great changes that always took place on a large organic farm.

Timothy and Timothina would have been very happy to have the wonderful cotton stay right where they were. The cotton tufts were beautiful, nourishing and fun. They had learned to play by bouncing on the cotton stem while holding onto the cotton.

They used the cotton to line their burrow so that

they had a wonderful soft place to sleep.

The cotton-harvesting machine was extremely large and powerful. It moved slowly through the cotton field, staying in line with the rows.

The cotton harvester was picking the cotton and converting the cotton into large bales while leaving the bare stems.

After the cotton harvester had finished, the field was very exposed. The leaves covered the ground and the stems of the cotton plants were bare and dried out. Only a few cotton tufts were left here and there.

Harvest always changed the farm a great deal, but this cotton harvest had left the field in an almost eerie condition with the dead dry cotton plants standing there like a desolate forest and huge cotton bales left in the field.

Mice always have to be very positive about life, so they carried on foraging in the hedgerow without letting the condition of the cotton field get to them. Timothina expressed their emotions best, upon the passing of the cotton field glory.

"Timothy, I look out now and all I see,

Is nothing like the way it used to be.

When we look out now, how does this seem?

In some way it reminds me of a scary dream.

The cotton plants were so interesting and new,

We learned so much as they grew.

Now with the newness gone,

Will there be something else to help us go on?"

# Dirt Bike

The mice had heard and seen the farm boy Will riding a noisy two-wheeled machine since the time of the pretty lights on the farmhouse. He liked to ride it in the morning before school and after school as well. He had an area next to the farmhouse where he would go tearing around and making his machine jump by going very fast over a mound of dirt.

He had always used his machine in the prescribed area, but with the cotton field dry and more open, the temptation was just too much for him. He started riding his dirt bike in the cotton field.

He would go through the cotton field as fast as he could down the furrows between the cotton bales. Timothy and Timothina, being adventuresome mice would run out into the cotton field when Will was riding his dirt bike just to watch him as he went flying through the field, knocking over dead cotton plants and dodging the huge bales. He seemed to be having so much fun, it picked up the mood of creatures out there among all of those dead cotton plants. Will did not know it, but the two mice would often race alongside of the two-wheeled machine, trying to see if they could stay ahead.

One afternoon after school, Will mounted his machine and took off.  The mice were ready.  They had really looked forward to Will getting home so they could play, with him on his dirt bike, in the dry cotton field.

As usual he rode his dirt bike for a while on the makeshift track next to the house. Then he made a sharp turn and out into the cotton field he came.  He usually rode his dirt bike along the side of the field next to the hedgerow, but today he went sailing off between the bales and right down the middle of the cotton field.

Find the important message in the cotton bale.

The mice ran out to join in the sport. With the machine making as much noise as it did and with Will there, they felt protected from predators. Will was not as well known to the mice as Lucina, but they had grown to like his very honest and direct way of playing. Also, they knew that he never tried to harm any of the farm animals, and he was very brave and adventurous.

On this particular day, Timothy was worried about Will because he knew that Will was speeding toward the ground squirrel mounds. Will was having a great time as he sped along.

Too late, he saw the ground squirrel mounds, overcorrected to miss a hole, and as he rode over the uneven ground created by the mounds, his bike wobbled terribly. Will tried to retain his balance, but it was no use. He crashed and his head hit hard against the ground.

Fortunately, he was wearing his helmet as his parents had told him to do, but he was knocked out.

He was laying there unconscious when his motor bike started to smoke. Timothina said,

"Brother dear, if we do not do something quick,

There is a sadness here that will forever stick.

This giant will be burned, I fear,

Because there are no giants that can help him near.

……………………………………..

Amelia's father said, "I think this is a good place to end this book."

Amelia who was very sleepy, suddenly woke up and cried out, "No, No, No, this book can't end here, I want to find out what happened to Will!"

Her father then said, "You will find out as soon as we start the next book."

"No," she said, "I Want to know what happens to him tonight, and besides I have a one-page coupon."

She then ceremoniously handed her father her imaginary one-page coupon, and of course, he said,

"Okay, one more page and that is it, but just in case you should fall asleep, please hand me the next book."

Amelia turned like she always did and picked up the imaginary book from her bookshelf. Her father took it and read the title to her, "Timothy the Sweet Potato Field Mouse." He pretended to sit the new book aside and in a very calm voice, read one last page of the "Cotton Field Mouse."

......................................

Timothy knew that the boy giant had to wake up and escape the machine. Where the dirt bike was smoking, a small flame shot up.

The mice were desperate; they had to do something or the boy giant could be burned to death. He had to wake up!

Then Timothy and Timothina just both seemed to understand what would give them their best chance to save the boy.

They turned together and ran back into the cotton field.

..........................................

Amelia's father looked over at his daughter. *She was asleep.*

# Interactive Chapter Guide:

## Mouse Dream

In this chapter Timothy's dream is crucial to help him see and prepare for the future. Just as in our lives, Timothy shares his dream with his wise and trusted friend, the pheasant, because by talking about his dream, he realizes he can gain a richer understanding of its meaning and better apply the lesson to his life.

Dreams put us in another world. Making images that are inspired by dreams can help us to understand our dreams better. Dreams can give us a glimpse into the future and they can help us to better deal with today. Try to remember your dreams. Write down your memories and make some drawings of dream imagery. Look for the hidden meanings in your dreams. Figuring out the importance of a dream can be like trying to solve a puzzle, but just as when you successfully solve a difficult puzzle, making a dream understandable and relevant can be both rewarding and fun.

There are many global websites that can be helpful in understanding dreams and symbols in dreams. This web site shares information about why it is important for parents to be a part of children's dreams: http://www.psychologytoday.com/blog/childs-play/201107/five-reasons-listen-your-childrens-dreams

# Animal Prejudice

The pheasants and the crows hate each other! But why? Is there a logical reason? And if not, is this a healthy thing?

The best way to understand prejudice is to break the word down into its component meanings: *pre* and *judge*. When we are prejudiced, we come to an assessment or opinion before we know the facts. We base our judgment on things that an animal or person is associated with rather than what they are as an individual, and that is why prejudice can limit our judgment and lead to terrible mistakes.

As an activity for this chapter, find someone or something that you really don't think that you could like but you don't know much about. Then investigate this person or thing in greater detail to see if you can discover reasons to change your opinion. I think you will be surprised how often a closer look will remove prejudice.

# Timothy Finds His Mother

All creatures have a mother, but having a mother and finding our mother can be two very different things. In this chapter *Timothy finds his mother which means he gets to know her.* He discovers, by talking to her and sharing with her, that she is a very different mouse from what he remembered as a mouseling. And because he understands her better, she becomes more real for him and more of a friend and partner, as well as a mother. As a result, their relationship takes on a very solid nature which it would not have, had she remained "just his mother."

As an activity for this chapter, let's "find" our mothers. Let's try to discover things about our mothers that we did not know, just as Timothy does with his mother. Then maybe (if we have not already done this), we can increase the bond between us *because we have "found" her.*

Another great activity for this chapter would be to draw a portrait of our mother. When we draw someone's face, often we reveal our inner feelings

about the person which can help us better understand the person we draw and ourselves, as well.  This website can get you started with basic proportions for a portrait drawing:
http://drawingfactory.hubpages.com/hub/portrait-drawing

# Ripper

We might call ripping the field the first very aggressive step that needs to be taken by our organic farmer in growing cotton.  The ripping plow is a beast of a tractor, they are scary enough for us humans, imagine how they must look to a mouse.  They can turn the soil to great depths.  Ripping is necessary because over time, the top foot or so of a field becomes overused; moreover, deeper plowing allows the irrigation water to penetrate farther into the soil.

Big tractors can be fun to watch and fun to draw.  Check out these pictures of ripping plows at work and find the plow you would like to use if you were ripping a farm field:
http://www.google.com/search?q=ripping+plows+at+work+images&oe=utf-8&aq=t&rls=org.mozilla:en-US:official&client=firefox-a&um=1&ie=UTF-8&hl=en&tbm=isch&source=og&sa=N&tab=wi&ei=TuhVUeHSJ4O49QTT5oGgDA&biw=1280&bih=638&sei=1utVUbfYNoeZ0QHgkIDIAg

# Disking

The large dirt clods and broken soil must be leveled and made softer to work with.  The disking plow breaks the large hunks of soil into finer pieces and then levels the planting field.

In this chapter, Timothy realizes how special Lucina is because she pays so much attention to the animals around her.  To make this chapter interactive, follow  Lucina's lead.  Pick an animal that is part of your environment and try to communicate with it.  Some great activities would be to train a dog, play a game with an animal or copy the sounds of a wild animal and see if you can get the wild animal to respond.   When an animal is trying to communicate, be responsive and try to figure out what it is saying.

# Fertilizer

Fertilizing a growing field is returning things that have been alive to the earth from which they came. In this way the recycling of organic matter gives new life. So, in a way this chapter is about cycles in nature, or you could say how everything living and dead is connected. The shaman in this chapter is a medium between the spirits of the living and the dead, so he is symbolic of the connection or interdependence of living things with things that lived before.

A great activity for this chapter would be to pick up a family album or pictorial history book and think about how your life is a continuation of the lives of your predecessors. Think of how we have learned from their lives and how they sometimes had to suffer in order to leave us the good things that we enjoy in our lives. When I illustrated this book, I was dependent on the pioneering agricultural artwork of Vincent Van Gogh. When you look at these pictures, I believe you will be able to see that connection: http://www.google.com/search?q=agricultural+art+of+vincent+van+gogh&hl=en&client=firefox-a&hs=6om&sa=X&rls=org.mozilla:en-US:official&channel=np&tbm=isch&tbo=u&source=univ&ei=AExWUZPXCvCw0QHvvoGACQ&ved=0CDMQsAQ&biw=1280&bih=638or you to Another great activity for this chapter would be to create your own agricultural art. You could even share your agricultural art with the Timothy community by posting it on Facebook at https://www.facebook.com/ on Timothy's page (search "Timothy the Cornfield Mouse").

# Listing up the Rows

The furrowing plow builds up the rows in preparation for planting the cotton. When Timothy seeks out first the wise old pheasant and then the trailer quail so he can find his sister, he illustrating how all living things need and depend on each other. As a chapter activity, pick any animal that you like

and think of how it is dependent on other types of animals. You could even draw a diagram that shows what animals your favorite animal is dependent on. There are some great resources that can help one learn about just how interrelated and dependent on one another all living things past and present are. Try these two to get started:
http://schools.bcsd.com/fremont/4th_sci_life_plant_animals.htm

http://www.learnnc.org/lp/pages/4214

# Deep Irrigation

Flooding the field in order to irrigate deeply is symbolic of the deep and enduring relationship that is developing between Timothy and his sister. The cotton will need water for the long hot dry summer therefore the irrigation must be deep so that the water will not evaporate too quickly.

Consistent with the theme of deep relationships is the introduction of Timothina's poetry. Make a poem of your own. Notice how when you write a poem you feel freer. When you read your poetical language don't be surprised if the words seem to have many layers of meaning because after all that's in many ways what poetry is all about. Writing a poem can also make you feel better and more in control:
http://www.telegraph.co.uk/culture/culturenews/4630043/AAAS-Writing-poems-helps-brain-cope-with-emotional-turmoil-say-scientists.html

# Pre-Planting-Irrigation

In order for seeds to germinate, there must be sufficient moisture close to the surface of the soil where the seeds are buried. Also, shallow irrigation is necessary for the decomposition of mulch. In this chapter the cotton field is flooded with surface water. Timothy knows that with the pre-irrigation, the giants are building the right conditions for monumental changes in the field that is his home.

He needs to discover more about the giants so that he can anticipate the changes and work for the harmony that is so important to the web of life on the farm.  To do this, he must cross the line between the wild world he is a part of and the domestic world of the giants.

When he enters Lucina's burrow, he sees many things that he cannot hope to understand.  He finds what he came for though, which is the understanding of the mystery of the root of prejudice.  He can see that it is embedded in the cultural-history of the wise old pheasant.  The pheasant comes from a very different background which makes him an alien.

The wise old pheasant's ancestors came from China where the history, religion and art are very different from the area where he is now living, and the crows have developed a prejudice against the "alien pheasants" simply because the crows lived in the area first and the pheasants are different.

Timothy realizes that his precious piece of jade with its green cross is a part of the culture as represented by Lucina's altar shelf and does not belong in the wild world that he is a part of.  He must return the jade in order to restore harmony between his wild world and the ideal world of the giants.  There is a very good description of the importance of jade in the Chinese culture on this website:
http://www.britishmuseum.org/explore/online_tours/asia/chinese_jade/chinese_jade.aspx

Do you have a piece of jade?  To make this chapter interactive, find some jade art.  Think of what it means as an individual piece and also what it means as part of the culture that it comes from.  The green cross represents a human-ideal connection to nature. To make this green cross interactive, you might find or make your own symbolic art to represent your very own ideal outlook toward nature.

# Mulching

Mulching accomplishes many things.  In order to retain moisture, mulch covers the soil to block the rays of the sun.  Some kinds of mulch can interact with the soil to add nutrients to promote healthier plants.   Mulch can even be effective in killing fungus, mold, weeds, and unwanted insects. There is an art to being able to mulch a field for best results, and sometimes mulching can create beautiful effects, such as changing the color of a plowed field, or creating beautiful textures. For proper mulching one must study the different kinds of mulch available and their applications to different kinds of crops. Mulch can be things like rocks, wood shavings, leaves, silage from a previous crop and artificial covers. Here are some web sites that let you see and read about mulch:

http://en.wikipedia.org/wiki/Mulch

http://www.nrcs.usda.gov/wps/portal/nrcs/detail/national/newsroom/features/?cid=nrcs143_023585

http://photobucket.com/images/mulching?page=1

In this chapter, Timothy is able to return the piece of jade, and this marks a new beginning in his life. By returning it to its rightful owner Timothy feels the loss of his treasured piece of jade, but he also feels a sense of freedom because he is no longer tied to its symbolic source or the power that it exerts on him. To make this chapter interactive, think of a time in your life when you returned something that you found and would have liked to keep. How did that make you feel?

## The Mulch Period

During the mulch period, the mulch does its work. It can be there to help retain moisture, kill insects, fertilize, and block the growth of harmful weeds. While the mulch work is going on, something very important develops concerning the animosity between the crows and the pheasants. Timothy confronts Gerald with what the wise old pheasant has told him about the crows stealing the pheasants' eggs. Gerald is very angry at first, and it looks like the friendship between Gerald and Timothy is in jeopardy. The tension is broken between Gerald and Timothy when Timothina uses a poem to bring the two friends to a better understanding, thus beginning a mending process between the crows and the pheasants. Poems can be very healing because getting your emotions on paper can help you to sort out what you are really feeling and just understanding in itself can be soothing. Make this chapter interactive by writing a poem about something that bothers you and see if that changes how you feel.

## Harrier Hawk

Aerial combat is something that happens all of the time in nature. In this chapter Gerald takes on a harrier hawk. The harrier hawk is much bigger and stronger than Gerald but also less maneuverable in the air. As long as Gerald can outmaneuver the hawk, he is safe. Make this chapter interactive by looking at some of the images of these amazing animals in flight and combat:

http://www.allaboutbirds.org/guide/Northern_Harrier/id

http://www.thebirdersreport.com/wild-birds/bird-sightings/red-tailed-hawk-attacked-by-crows

## Cotton Planting

When any crop is planted, it is a special time of change. The sowing of a new crop initiates the cycle of growth. A cotton crop must be planted when the combination of the daytime and nighttime temperatures are over 100 degrees Fahrenheit. The cotton seeds will produce little plants in about five days if everything is just right, i.e., nutrient-rich soil, enough moisture and sunlight, and the temperatures are warm enough.

Check out these tractors planting the cotton in nice rows that are evenly spaced:

http://library.thinkquest.org/5443/images/cotton6.jpg

http://www.agweb.com/assets/1/10/GalleryMainDimensionId/16B124DHi%20res1.PNG

The farmer is already thinking of the harvest and needs to have the rows just the right distance apart for the harvesting machine:

## Moonlight and Friendship

In this chapter, the magic of moonlight brings good friends together to work on saving another friend (the wise old pheasant). The beauty and harmony of the moonlight created special effects in the night. Take an evening walk and look for the beauty of the scenery in the moonlight. Notice how colors are affected by the moonlight. They will appear much softer and muted. Maybe you could make a moonlight picture of your own using the information that you have gained by walking and exploring by the light of the moon.

http://media02.hongkiat.com/moonbow-photography/double-moonbow-in-dorgali.jpg

http://www.artfromthesoul.com/Moonbow.jpg

http://upload.wikimedia.org/wikipedia/commons/thumb/c/cb/Lunar_Rainbow_3_-_ORION_L_-_Victoria_Falls_-_Calvin_Bradshaw_3.jpg/300px-Lunar_Rainbow_3_-_ORION_L_-_Victoria_Falls_-_Calvin_Bradshaw_3.jpg

http://vortex.accuweather.com/adc2004/pub/includes/columns/newsstory/2011/590x393_07151450_moonbow_brian_hawkins_72.jpg


# Screech Owl

The screech owl is an amazing night predator. Their ability to see at night is way beyond that of us humans; their hearing is also vastly superior to ours, and their plumage also conceals them at night. Predators are extremely important in nature because without them, the populations of their prey animals would become far too numerous. Predators also make their prey animals stronger since those most able to survive will pass on their characteristics to succeeding generations and thus improve the species.

Look at the screech owls. Notice that there are eastern and western varieties of screech owls in the United States:
http://www.wallpaperpimper.com/wallpaper/download-wallpaper-Western_Screech_Owl_Montana-size-1024x768-id-121811.htm

# Cotton Squares

The first part of the cotton plant that will become the cotton is the beginning of the flower which is called a "square." The squares start off unbelievably tiny. It is at this stage that the cotton is at its greatest risk from insects. There are many different kinds of insects that can attack the square and destroy a cotton crop. The most famous insect to ever attack cotton was the boll weevil. Make this chapter interactive by drawing your own boll weevil. Here are some really cool images of the boll weevil and the Boll Weevil Monument in Enterprise, Alabama:

http://en.wikipedia.org/wiki/File:Boll_weevil_monument.jpg

http://ipm.ncsu.edu/cotton/insectcorner/photos/images/Adult_boll_weevil.jpg

http://4.bp.blogspot.com/_VhVnQirjpOo/SCWcAZKTPFI/AAAAAAAAAXk/U6_a9jaR9zQ/s400/boll+weevil.jpg

# Cotton Flowers

When the cotton flowers bloom the cotton world turns white and cream-colored with a magnificent fragrance all of its own. Bees are buzzing and the world is beautiful. Timothy does not know how his brown color will upset the bees. Could it be that there is a much larger brown mammal whose brown color could cause the bees to react to Timothy?

Look at these cotton flower and great beekeeper images and see why Timothy's color may have upset the bees. This chapter can be made interactive by tasting "cotton blossom honey." After tasting cotton blossom honey you will understand why Timothy was so attracted to its scent.

http://www.alohafriendsphotos.com/web%20art/Hawaiian_cotton_flower_004.jpg

http://www.coralreefphotos.com/wp-content/uploads/2012/01/cotton-flower-2.jpg

http://lubbockonline.com/local-news/2012-09-11/cotton-yields-honey-blossom-and-cooking-oil-seeds#.UunNKvsTnSg

http://cdn.ph.upi.com/sv/em/upi/UPI-38491350318486/2012/1/e35ebe9f4d54bbc163ab406cbfbb2e51/Bears-steal-100-pounds-of-honey.jpg

http://i2.cdnds.net/12/42/618x445/odd_honey_bee.jpg

http://upload.wikimedia.org/wikipedia/commons/thumb/4/4c/Beekeeper_keeping_bees.jpg/250px-Beekeeper_keeping_bees.jpg

http://i.dailymail.co.uk/i/pix/2010/06/02/article-0-09D77AB1000005DC-897_468x384.jpg

http://therealnewsjournal.com/wp-content/uploads/2010/12/BeeKeeperAPEX_468x310.jpg

# Cotton Bolls

Healthy cotton bolls mean that the future looks bright for the cotton crop. When Lucina and her father inspect the bolls and find them healthy, there is a real sense of relief that insects like the boll weevil have not damaged the crop and their organic remedies to the boll weevil infestation have been successful.   Are there other plants that have bolls?   Look at these milkweed bolls and leaves. They look very much like cotton bolls and even produce a type of cotton.   Could the milkweed plant be an ancient relative of the domestic cotton plant?

The monarch butterfly is sometimes called the milkweed butterfly because their life cycle is tied so closely to the milkweed.  The toxic chemistry of the milkweed that the monarch butterfly ingests keeps it safe from predators, and the monarchs help pollinate the milkweed flowers.   Look at the images of monarch butterflies on the milkweed.   The interdependent relationship of the milkweed and the monarch butterfly is a great example of why it is important to protect the diversity of plant and animal life.

http://www.inmagine.com/imb013/imb0130527-photo

http://upload.wikimedia.org/wikipedia/commons/thumb/0/00/Milkweed-in-seed2.jpg/190px-Milkweed-in-seed2.jpg

http://www.nwf.org/~/media/Content/NWM/Gardening/Limited-Rights/Pollinator-Plants/monarchs_PatriciaAWood_570x363.jpg?w=570&h=363&as=1

http://npsot.org/wp/wp-content/uploads/2009/06/monarch-texas-milkweed-300.jpg

# Cotton

How thrilling it is for Timothy and Timothina to find the first cotton fibers.  It has been very challenging for the organic cotton farmers and the mice alike to get to this glorious point.

Cotton fibers form around the seeds of the boll.  They are used to make fabric, twine, thread, paper, soft fillings for toys and pillows, and medical swabs.  Cotton fibers are also used industrially for their very adaptable cellulous chemistry.   Look at these articles and images for the many uses of cotton fibers.  A great idea for making your own images might be to make a drawing or painting that illustrates how cotton fibers can be changed into so many useful things.

http://media.treehugger.com/assets/images/2011/10/H26M_Organic_and_Recycled_Cotton_Clothing.jpg

http://wanttoknowit.com/uses-of-cotton/

http://i.huffpost.com/gen/555982/thumbs/s-NEW-USES-COTTON-BALLS-large640.jpg

# Ground Squirrels

The California ground squirrel lives in areas where the soil is dry. When the cotton field became very dry, the ground squirrels were attracted to this habitat. Here again we see the conflict between the wilderness world and the domestic world of agriculture. The California ground squirrel is a threat to the cotton farm because the ground squirrels will destroy plants, and they can invade the farmhouse and literally undermine its foundation. Also, it is possible that they can carry a deadly disease known as bubonic plague. Because our organic farmers in this story do not want to use poisons or kill traps to control the infestation of ground squirrels, they try to harmonize the needs of the farm with the needs of wild animals by moving the ground squirrels to a designated wilderness area where their population size is controlled by natural predators.

The California ground squirrel is a really amazing animal. They have a legendary ability to make tunnel networks even through very hard rocky soil. They are extremely aggressive and fearless as well. Read some of the articles and take a look at some of these images online that illustrate the beauty and abilities of the California ground squirrel. They are fun to draw (be sure and show their very strong muscles). One of their primary predators is the rattlesnake. However, the ground squirrels are so smart, they have developed techniques for escaping the rattlesnake.

http://en.wikipedia.org/wiki/California_ground_squirrel

http://www.nhptv.org/natureworks/californiagroundsquirrel.htm

http://www.earthweek.com/online/ew071221/ew071221g.jpg

http://www.activelightphotography.com/Pictures/Wildlife/Mammals/Squirrels%20-%20Ground/DML-GS-CA0234.jpg

http://www.majestyofbirds.com/w_bobcatgroundsquirrel_lrg.jpg

# Rex

In this chapter Rex symbolizes the importance of predators in keeping a balance in nature. Rex is highly intelligent as all predator species must be. Rex makes an exception for the two mice that join him in the celebration of the moon. The coyote is such an intelligent animal that they have been successful in living in almost any habitat.

We usually only equate individuality as a human trait, which is utterly false. Animals have individual personalities just like humans, and this allows Rex to take the extraordinary step of befriending Timothy and Timothina. This friendship of predator and prey is highly unusual but entirely possible and necessary for Timothy and Timothina to keep moving forward in their purpose. Friendship based on individual uniqueness is a great source of strength. For this chapter, think of some unusual friendships that you have known of between animals and perhaps make a picture to illustrate the relationship. Look at these Internet images that illustrate these types of odd animal friendships:

http://megaodd.com/wp-content/uploads/2011/06/Unusual-friendship-between-animals-11.jpg

http://designyoutrust.com/wp-content/uploads/2012/02/168.jpg

http://megaodd.com/wp-content/uploads/2011/06/Unusual-friendship-between-animals-09.jpg

http://static.guim.co.uk/sys-images/Lifeandhealth/Pix/pictures/2012/2/3/1328265669470/The-macaque-and-the-dove-002.jpg

http://l.yimg.com/ea/img/-/120911/elephant_cat_184ssbj-184ssdi.jpg?x=400&q=80&n=1&sig=fk4fCp3ZxhNghQFUlG4rfw--

http://xaxor.com/images/other/111138/Friendship_03.jpg

# Defoliant

When the defoliant is used on the cotton plant, the plant's annual life is pretty much over. The defoliant knocks the leaves off of the plant so that the harvesting machine can pick the cotton with less material to get in the way of separating the cotton from the rest of the dry plant. In an organic cotton farm, organic chemicals are used to remove the extra leaves from the plant. The use of organic chemicals is important because they do not leave residues in the soil that can build up over the years and render the soil unfit for growing crops, or leave unhealthy residues in the cotton fibers.

In this chapter the mice discover the *cotton seed*. They find the cotton seeds nutritious, and indeed they are. Cotton seeds are used for many kinds of human food and industrial products. To make this chapter interactive, buy some cotton seed oil and try it for cooking. It has zero trans fat and is very good for frying foods such as potato chips.

http://janiceperson.com/agriculture/animal-ag/cotton-101-cotton-seed-uses/

http://www.ehow.com/list_6088461_uses-cotton-seed.html

http://en.wikipedia.org/wiki/Cottonseed_oil

# Dry Cotton

The cotton is dry now and ready to harvest. It is also the time of the pheasant hunt. Sunny the hunting dog is ready, or is he? William Shakespeare wrote "the best laid plans of mice and men often go awry." This was one of those times because the mice were able to save the wise old pheasant by distracting Sunny with the tennis ball and thus, the hunters' plans were foiled. Are we humans the only ones who can make plans and carry them out?

I think not! Let's read about some animal planning:

http://abcnews.go.com/Health/Healthday/story?id=7039683&page=1#.UXRhF2P4IRM

http://www.livescience.com/4393-birds-humans-plan.html

# Cotton Harvest

The cotton harvest is both a celebratory and a sad time. It brings to a successful completion all of the hard work and trials of the farmers and animals, but on the other hand, it takes away the world that the animals knew and had become used to.  The cotton field world, as Timothina said, "The cotton plants were so interesting and new,

We learned so much as they grew.

Now with the newness gone,

Will there be something else to help us go on?"

The baled cotton will eventually be loaded onto trucks and taken to the gin. The cotton gin that separates the cotton from the cotton seeds was first invented by Eli Whitney in 1793.  Make this chapter interactive by looking at some websites that have information and images of the cotton gin:

http://en.wikipedia.org/wiki/Cotton_gin

http://americanenterprise.si.edu/wp-content/uploads/2012/01/WhitneyCottonGin.jpg

http://www.socialstudiesforkids.com/graphics/cottongin.jpg

http://www.cottoninc.com/product/NonWovens/Nonwoven-Technical-Guide/Agricultural-Production/Cottongin.jpg

http://mavensphotoblog.com/wp-content/uploads/2012/10/Cotton-gin-Oct-2012-1.jpg

# Dirt Bike

It's kind of predictable that something less than ideal would happen right at the end of a cotton field book.  That seems to be just the way things go with cotton and again the brave but impulsive young Will would be just the one you would expect to get into trouble in the cotton field.  Will he be alright? Well, I don't think you should worry too much; after all, he has Timothy and Timothina trying to save him.

Do animals save people?  Yes, it happens all of the time.

http://www.mnn.com/earth-matters/animals/photos/10-remarkable-animals-that-have-saved-lives/willie-the-parrot-gives-the

Made in the USA
Middletown, DE
14 May 2022